MURDER AT VOLCANO HOUSE

A Surfing Detective Mystery

Other Surfing Detective Books
by Chip Hughes

MURDER ON MOLOKA'I

WIPEOUT! & HANGING TEN IN PARIS

KULA

SURFING DETECTIVE

CONFIDENTIAL INVESTIGATIONS : ALL ISLANDS

MURDER AT VOLCANO HOUSE

A Surfing Detective Mystery

CHIP HUGHES

SLATE RIDGE PRESS

SLATE RIDGE PRESS

P.O. Box 1886
Kailua, HI 96734
slateridgepress@hawaii.rr.com

ISBN: 0982944446
ISBN-13: 9780982944448

First Edition, 2014

In the time-honored tradition of fiction writing, the author has taken artistic liberties in the depiction of certain sights, facilities, and geographic features. The hotel of the book's title is not intended to be the Volcano House of today. The hotel was shuttered when the story was written and on-site research was conducted a decade earlier when flames of the old hotel's famous fireplace still flickered. And, of course, characters that populate the story are products of imagination rather than actual persons.

Cover photo: Alan Cressler, Halemaʻumaʻu Crater

"Even from a mile away I can see the smoke—a massive column spiraling into the sunset sky."

Acknowledgements

Many thanks once again to my wife, collaborator, and inspiration, Charlene, and to brilliant and extraordinarily generous Honolulu private detective Stu Hilt. *Mahalo* to Sher Glass, President, Volcano Community Association; to Doug Crispin, National Park Service ranger and long-ago CSU-Chico housemate; to John Broward, Emergency Operations Coordinator and Eruption Crew Supervisor, Hawai'i Volcanoes National Park; to Christine Matthews, consummate mystery editor and Secretary, Private Eye Writers of America; and to Doug Corleone, whose fast-moving narratives I've tried to emulate. For editorial suggestions and proofreading, I'm grateful to Nathan Avallone, Les Peetz, Laurie Tomchak, and Lorna Hershinow. Finally, special thanks to Alan Cressler for the cover photo of Halema'uma'u Crater.

Holmes: "There is a realm in which the most acute and most experienced of detectives is helpless."

Watson: "You mean that the thing is supernatural?"

—*The Hound of the Baskervilles,* Arthur Conan Doyle

one

It's Friday afternoon in late March—one of those mild and calm days in Honolulu when coconut palms outside my office above Fujiyama's Flower Leis barely whisper in the slack trade winds. I'm about to close up shop and paddle out to Pops in Waikīkī.

My phone rings. *Maile?*

No such luck. Caller ID says: TOMMY WOO. Attorney-at-law, jazz pianist, jokester, and friend.

"Howzit, Tommy?" I answer.

"Hey, Kai," he says, "how do you get a lawyer out of a banyan tree?"

"If I knew, Tommy, you'd tell me anyway." There's no stopping him.

Tommy is quiet for a moment. Then he says: "Cut the rope."

"That's it?" I ask.

What a mistake. A barrage of blue ones follow.

When the jokes finally end I say, "What can I do for you, Tommy?"

"I've got a customer for you."

"A paying customer?"

"Absolutely," he says. "And she needs your services now."

"Now? As in immediately? I'm on my way out the door."

"You don't need to start until Monday. But she wants to see you today—to make arrangements."

"Arrangements for what?"

"She'll explain. She's here in my office. Well, she just stepped out when I called you. She wants me to come with her."

There goes surfing!

"How soon can you get here?" I glance at the clock on my desk. It's already four. I want to be in the water in twenty minutes.

"Give us fifteen," Tommy says.

"It's got to be a short meeting, Tommy. I have to be somewhere at four thirty."

"I'll bet you do," he says. He knows my ways.

"Who is the woman?" I ignore his sarcasm. "She a client of yours?"

"Never met her before. She lives on Kāua'i. But I recognized her and you will too. I did some work for her husband a long time ago—before she married him. Anyway, that's how she found me. Being married to him, she's got money. And the case will take you to a neighbor island. 'SURFING DETECTIVE: CONFIDENTIAL INVESTIGATIONS—ALL ISLANDS,' like your card says. Eh, Kai?"

"A case on Kāua'i?"

"No, on the Big Island."

Now I'm really confused, so I simply say, "I'm already working a case—that Pali Highway crash."

"Tragic," Tommy says, revealing his softer side. "I feel for those girls' parents."

"Me too. Actually, I'm waiting on some things and can spare a day or two. But that's all."

"Perfect," Tommy says. "A few days are all you'll need. I'll bring her over."

two

While I wait for Tommy and the mystery woman whose name he assures me I'll recognize, I dial Maile's home number. Maile probably won't pick up, so I work out a message for her in my head. I've given up calling her cell phone. I guess trust is one of those things that's easy to lose and hard to recover.

Her home phone rings and then her machine kicks in. "Hi, this is Maile Barnes, tracer of missing pets. How can I help?"

"Maile, it's Kai." I start to spew out my rehearsed message: "I wondered if you wanted me to take Kula surfing again. It's been a while and I haven't heard from you—I mean, Kula hasn't been in the water—unless . . ." I'm wandering, so I try to get back on course. "Well, I can take him Sunday . . . Uh, just let me know. Call me, text me, email me. Whatevahs."

I had a crush on Maile in high school. When I was off to college, she married someone else, became a K9 cop, and then, suddenly, a young widow. She quit the force and started a pet detective agency.

Recently Maile helped me on a case. We hit it off like a house on fire. She warned me never to cheat on her, since she'd been burned before. I didn't, exactly. But my explanations have fallen on deaf ears. Now she won't speak to me—except about Kula. Kula is the golden retriever she helped me rescue for one of my former clients. She's fostering the dog, since my client is unavoidably detained. He's spending the rest of his life in jail.

I gaze out my office window onto Maunakea Street's *lei* shops, dim sum parlors, fish markets, vegetable stalls, and art galleries, whiff the sweet odors and reeks wafting up, and wonder why I'm so stuck on Maile. Is it because the spunky ex-cop and I are so much alike—that old-fashioned romantic notion of soul mates? Or because I'm still haunted by her soft curves and jasmine-scented sheets?

I don't come up with an answer before there's a knock at the door. Tommy steps in, adjusts his tortoiseshell glasses, sweeps back a lock of silver hair, and gestures to the woman next to him. "Kai Cooke, meet Donnie Ransom."

I draw a blank on her name. But I do vaguely recognize her face. When Tommy announces—"Miss Hawai'i finalist"—I know why.

"My name was Lam then," she says. "Not Ransom. That was twenty years ago."

It's coming back to me now. Donnie Lam was not just a finalist, but first runner-up. Though she missed the crown by a sliver back then, she strides into my office with the grace and elegance of a reigning beauty queen. Her hair is long, lustrous and black; her eyes sparkle like agates in the sun. She wears more mascara and brighter red lipstick than I'd say is necessary for a daytime meeting with an attorney, but they make her eyes and smile all the more vivid.

Tommy says: "She has a job for you."

I expect to hear what sort of job, but she seems more interested in the locale.

"On the Big Island," Mrs. Ransom says, "at Hawai'i Volcanoes National Park." Leaving Tommy standing, she takes the one extra chair in my office. "We'll put you up at the Volcano House, all expenses paid."

"The Volcano House?" I say. "There's nothing like sleeping on the edge of an active crater."

Tommy smiles and so does Mrs. Ransom. I look at her more closely. She has that harmonious blend of Hawaiian, Asian and *haole,* or Caucasian, we call local girl. There are only a few visible hints of the two decades that have passed since she almost became Miss Hawai'i: faint lines around her eyes and mouth, and a little fullness in her neck and figure.

"Like I told Tommy, Mrs. Ransom, I'm working another case at the moment and can spare only a few days."

"Please call me Donnie," she says. "And don't worry, we'll have you back on O'ahu by Tuesday evening. Wednesday morning, at the very latest."

"That might work," I say.

"I'm so glad." Her youthful complexion glows against her black silk dress. Tommy, also in black, as usual, looks rumpled by comparison.

"Now just what is it exactly you'd like me to do?" I ask.

She perks up. "I want you to come with my husband and me to the Volcano House. To—sort of—chaperone him."

"That's it?" *Did I miss something?*

"Let me explain. My husband is Rex Ransom. You may have heard his name. Rex was founder and CEO of Ransom Geothermal, a drilling operation on the Big Island in the Wao Kele O Puna rainforest. Rex pulled out of there years ago and sold the company."

"I remember him," I say. But I don't like what I remember. I've got nothing against geothermal energy—and other alternatives to burning foreign oil—but what this man did was something else.

"Rex and I are going to the Big Island for the funeral of his former corporate attorney, Stan Nagahara. Stan died recently in the national park and his service will take place at the military camp chapel there. He's the second from Rex's company to die there in as many years. Stan's death was no accident. Neither was Karl Krofton's two years ago. They were both killed by Pele."

"Excuse me," I say. "Do you mean Madame Pele, the goddess of fire and volcanoes?"

"Exactly. Pele's going to take revenge on Rex, just like she did on the other two."

I try to keep a straight face, but it's tough, because behind Mrs. Ransom, Tommy is cracking a smile. So I say: "Why do you think Pele took revenge on those two, and plans to do the same to your husband?"

"Pele's followers believe that by drilling in the rainforest Rex and his company violated and desecrated her. They believe what Ransom Geothermal did amounted to rape. I'm afraid they're right. And if Rex puts himself in Pele's domain, she will strike him down."

"What makes you think those other two were killed by Pele?"

"There's no doubt. Look at these." Mrs. Ransom hauls out two newspaper clippings, one slightly faded, the other newer, whiter. She hands me the faded one first—from two years ago in the Hilo newspaper.

I read it aloud, in case Tommy also needs bringing up to speed.

Clues Sought in Volcano Accident

Hawai'i Volcanoes National Park: Park Service rangers are asking residents and visitors in the Volcano area to provide information about an accident that left former Ransom Geothermal executive Karl Kroften dead. Kroften's crushed BMW was found Thursday morning by a park visitor. The car had apparently careened off Crater Rim Drive near the Halema'uma'u Crater, flipped, and landed on its roof in a hardened lava bed. Speed may have been a factor. Kroften had no prior accidents, traffic citations, or arrests. He was known to friends and former co-workers as a quiet man who lived alone, enjoyed motor sports, and did not drink.

Earlier that evening a park visitor reported seeing a grey-haired woman smoking a cigarette climb into a silver BMW sedan like Kroften's with a white dog. When the wrecked car was recovered, no trace of the old woman or her dog was found. Volcano residents familiar with the legend of Pele say that what the park visitor saw was the fire goddess in one of her many *kinolau* or guises.

"You see," Mrs. Ransom says, "Karl Kroften's death was the work of Pele. It couldn't be clearer. Pele has the *mana*—the power—to take many forms. That's what *kinolau* means. *Kino* is Hawaiian for body and *lau* for many."

Tommy raises his brows.

I say something vaguely neutral like, "Uh-huh." And then, "Or maybe he was driving too fast?"

"Rex says Karl was an excellent driver," she goes on. "Rex rode with him many times to job sites. No, it was Pele."

Then she hands me a week-old clipping from the Honolulu daily.

Volcano Attorney Found Dead in East Rift Zone

Hilo: Big Island attorney Stanley Nagahara, who once represented Ransom Geothermal Enterprises, was found dead yesterday in an inactive lava tube in the East Rift Zone in Hawai'i Volcanoes National Park. A search and rescue effort began late Tuesday evening when Nagahara, who had been hiking alone, failed to return home. His body was discovered early Wednesday morning in a crevasse of nearly one hundred feet into which he had apparently tumbled. Family members and friends were at a loss to explain the accident. Nagahara was an avid and experienced hiker who often explored lava tubes and caves in

> the area. He is the second former Ransom
> Geothermal executive to die accidentally
> in Hawai'i Volcanoes National Park in as
> many years. Two years ago drilling engi-
> neer Karl Kroften died in a single car acci-
> dent near the Halema'uma'u Crater . . .

"It's a pattern," she says. "Rex would be the third. Bad things come in threes. He's Pele's next victim."

"A car accident . . . a fallen hiker . . . two years apart," I reply. "How is that a pattern?"

"Pele makes the pattern. She's behind it all. Both deaths happened in her domain—on her *'aina*. Both involved high-ranking people in Rex's company. This is her revenge. But the one she wants most is Rex. He was the head of the whole operation."

"Two high-ranking officials from your husband's company have died, out of how many?" I try to be the voice of reason. "Isn't it just a coincidence?"

"I'm not willing to take that chance," she replies. "I wish Rex wouldn't attend the funeral, but Stan was his friend as well as his corporate attorney. They endured a lot together. Rex says he must go and pay his respects."

"I have to admit," I say, "I was sympathetic back then to Hawaiians who opposed drilling in their rainforest." Images surface in my memory from the news coverage of Ransom's crews and their machinery ripping and scarring the frag-ile forest. The ongoing protests could do nothing to stop the devastation.

"I was sympathetic too," she says.

"In good conscience," I hear myself say, "I don't see how I can go with you."

Tommy frowns.

I'm hoping the conversation will end here.

three

The conversation doesn't end.

Donnie Ransom's beauty queen smile tightens. She pushes on, sounding desperate now.

"I promise you—Rex is a changed man. He's beginning to feel his own mortality. He had a heart attack back in September. And two days of tests last month at Wilcox Hospital confirmed he could have another. It's been so hard."

"It must be difficult for you." I try to be sympathetic.

"I went to Lāna'i while he was in the hospital. Caregivers have to take care of themselves, you know." Donnie keeps going. "Rex has developed a fear of Pele. He has nightmares about her in her various guises—beautiful young woman in red, old lady in white, and so on. He wakes up screaming. Believe me, he's not the hard-charging conservative from Montana he was thirty years ago. He's even renting our guest quarters to an openly gay man."

"Why don't you have your renter escort you and your husband?" I say, still looking for a way out.

"Jeffrey? Oh, I don't think Jeffrey could protect anyone. He's a lovely, sensitive man, but . . ." She hesitates. "He's boarding the *Pride of Aloha* this Saturday with his friend, Byron, for a week-long inter-island cruise."

"Why don't you hire a Big Island PI?" I try again. "You won't have to pay travel expenses."

"Money is no object," she says. "Besides I don't know anybody on the Big Island. And Mr. Woo says I can trust you."

Tommy winks. I know what that means. The Ransoms could bring him more business, if I do well. Plus I owe him. Tommy helped me recover Kula, the golden retriever Maile is now fostering. I glance at my attorney friend again and see the writing on the wall.

"I'll pay your room, airfare, car, everything, plus your daily fees," she says. "All you have to do is follow my husband at a safe distance and make sure nothing happens to him. He's proud and wouldn't hear of being protected, so you'll have to do it incognito."

"Incognito?" I'm surprised she knows the word. But what she apparently doesn't know is that following someone unnoticed is not easy, especially in the wide-open spaces of a national park. If you're far enough away not to be seen, you may be too far to protect the client from sudden violence. The job is nearly impossible.

"That's right," she says. "I'll keep in touch with you when I can by cell phone and let you know our movements."

Tommy gives me a look.

It's only a few days, I rationalize. *And I won't have to be seen with the man.*

"Okay," I hear myself say.

When Tommy and the woman finally leave my office and clear the building I rush out right behind them. I can almost smell the waves.

I don't get far. At the bottom of the stairs I see Blossom, one of Mrs. Fujiyama's *lei* girls, crying. She's a slim, sweet local girl, barely out of high school. Mrs. Fujiyama is looking distressed, but doing nothing. Chastity and Joon, her other *lei* girls, are sitting stock-still.

I see what the problem is. Blossom's boyfriend—or her ex-boyfriend—Junior has tracked her down at work. He's got his big mitt on her and he isn't letting go. Blossom tries to pull away. That makes Junior clutch on harder. He's about twice her size. And he must outweigh me.

"You're hurting me," she cries. She's broken up with him before, but he just won't go away.

Mrs. Fujiyama tells Junior if he doesn't leave she's going to call the police.

I'm standing on the stairs, looking down on this. *What can I do?* Punks like Junior are bad news—they punch first and talk later. I can handle him, if it comes to that. But I don't want to antagonize him, unless I have to. He starts flinging Blossom around like a ragdoll and Mrs. Fujiyama screams she's going to call.

That's it. I can't watch any more. I step down and say, "No need. I'll call." I pull out my cellphone, look directly at Junior, and dial 911.

The line rings and rings. Finally an operator answers.

"Police," I say. "Emergency." I keep looking at Junior, wondering if he's coming for me.

There's a bit of a wait before a dispatcher gets on the line. I hold the phone to my ear, never taking my eyes off the punk. He's not pulling Blossom now. In fact, he's let go of her. I suspect there's a warrant out on him, or he's on parole, because he's starting to look uneasy.

Finally, I get a dispatcher.

"Assault in progress," I say. "Corner of Maunakea and Beretania. Fujiyama's Flower Leis."

The dispatcher asks me what's happening. But before I can answer, Junior is hustling out the door. He turns back and flips me the bird. "I get you, fuckah!"

After things calm down in the *lei* shop, I give HPD my version of events in a witness statement. Then I head for the beach.

Junior, it turns out, does have outstanding warrants. But they've never been served. There's a backlog of warrants in the City and County of Honolulu and not enough personnel to serve them. So guys like Junior sometimes go on their merry way.

Me, I've got enough on my plate already without dealing with him. There's the Pali case, not to mention that Big Island errand I'd rather not think about. But as I cruise down Maunakea Street with the nose of my board riding on my Impala's dash, the brown haze hanging in the dying afternoon sky won't let me forget.

It's vog—volcanic smog—drifting up from the Big Island and signaling another eruption in the East Rift Zone. Volcanoes down there have been going off sporadically for months. Red-hot molten lava flowing to the sea brings out the crowds. The Volcano House will be busy.

It's sunset when I finally paddle out to Pops. Usually I can leave my cases on shore, if I choose, but the vog keeps me in mind of Rex Ransom. No way I'd work for the man—ever—except to repay a favor. I'm hoping the waves will let me forget. At least, temporarily.

As I'm paddling to the lineup I glance back at the Sheraton Waikīkī, soaring directly opposite the break. In old times, many Hawaiians lived on the oceanfront land the hotel now occupies. They named the surf spot offshore of their home Populars, because it was a favorite break in the area. There's a reason, beyond proximity, why it was popular with Hawaiians back then, and remains popular with surfers today. Though we call it simply Pops.

On a good day, Pops serves up long, hollow, right-breaking curls that you can ride almost forever. As the wave peels and swings toward shore, it often bowls in sections. A couple hundred yards offshore, and far from the more accessible Waikīkī breaks, Pops is a long paddle from anywhere. And that keeps the crowds small and mellow, except during a big south swell.

Then look out. The waves are packed, the riders more aggressive, and the vibe more edgy. On one of those big days a hotshot once ran right over the top of my board—slicing my deck with his skeg. Then he had the gall to ask if he could see the damage he'd done. I covered the scar with my prone body and told him he didn't hit me after all. He paddled away looking disappointed.

As the sun sinks in the west, the brown haze on the horizon turns glittering gold. A few riders are paddling in, and a few dozen remain. Friday afternoon. *Pau hana*—quitting time. I should've known. I don't like crowds, even small crowds, so I paddle next door in the *Ewa* direction to the peaky breaks of Paradise. There I'm one of only three surfers. The waves are fewer and farther between, but when they jack up there's plenty for everybody.

In between rides, thoughts of Rex Ransom return. Sherlock Holmes had his pipe—I have my surfboard. Floating on the glassy sea, scanning the horizon for my next wave, sometimes I can solve problems that elude me on shore. Out of the blue I recall memories from the distant past. Ransom's controversial drilling operation at Wao Kele O Puna and the disputed land swap that enabled it made him a very unpopular man, especially among Hawaiians and members of the SPC— Save Pele Coalition. They believed Ransom had despoiled the rainforest—essential to their cultural practices and gathering rights—and defiled, if not raped, their goddess. I can't say I fully understand the depth of their belief in Pele and other Hawaiian deities. But it's hard to miss her power among her followers.

Donnie Ransom knows the score. But she's worried only about Pele—not about the protesters who had tried to defend her. Their revenge seems more likely than hers. My prospective job is looking hairier by the minute. It's tough enough to fend off a goddess—not to mention a raft of mortal foes. Better find out more about Ransom's human enemies before catching my flight to Hilo on Monday.

I glance out to sea. Here comes another Paradise roller. The wave builds and peaks like a liquid pyramid. I swing my board around, paddle, and rise. The drop is steep and fast. I make my turn. *Stoked!* Before I know it, the ride is over.

I pivot my board around and paddle back to the lineup, smiling ear to ear. I try to remember what I was thinking about. *Rex who?*

four

Saturday morning, on my way to the Pali Highway, I pass by the Aloha Tower. The big white cruise ship *Pride of Aloha* is moored just to the right of the tower. Above its flower-festooned bow and soaring stack the brown haze of vog from the Big Island still hangs in the air. I remember Donnie Ransom saying that their renter will board the ship tonight for the weeklong inter-island cruise. I'd like to trade places with Jeffrey. Let me take the cruise and him shadow his landlord. All my years in the islands—born and raised—I've never been on one of those ships.

"You're not the cruise type, Kai." I hear Tommy Woo's sardonic voice in my ear. Tommy may be right. But I imagine myself gazing from a porthole onto the sunlit sea. *Nah.*

I shrug it off and aim my old Chevy up the Pali Highway toward the windward side of O'ahu. My Impala's big V-8 growls up the highway, called Route 61 on the map, climbing through lush Nu'uanu Valley to the tunnels at the *pali,* or cliff. Beyond the tunnels, the *pali* drops more than one thousand feet.

The sheer plunge has caused many deaths, some long before the three I'm investigating today. The first road was built back in 1845 over an ancient Hawaiian footpath that carefully navigated the cliff. When the second was blazed in 1898, hundreds of skulls were found, believed to be the remains of warriors who jumped or were forced from the cliff when Kamehameha I conquered the island of O'ahu. The present highway replaced the old road in 1959 and introduced the tunnels where the accident I'm working on occurred.

Even as I pursue the Pali case, thoughts of Pele keep intruding. *Da goddess stay* pa'a *in my mind!* Just before I reach the ramp to the scenic Pali Lookout—with its sweeping views of the Windward coast—I remember the story about Pele preventing cars from passing through these tunnels. Motorists reported their vehicles mysteriously stopping and not starting again—until they removed pork they were packing. *Lolo?* Not in Hawaiian legend. The goddess once intercepted a half human, half hog god named Kamapua'a and did not allow him, or any form of pork thereafter, to pass. Since I've got no bacon on board, my Chevy glides through the tunnels without incident.

Not so for those unfortunates involved in the case I'm working. On the Windward side of the tunnels, about a week ago, a Honda Civic plunged from the cliff and landed upside down, killing everyone aboard—the driver, Freddie "Fireball" Furman, and his two passengers, twin sisters Heather and Lindsay Lindquist. The twins had been celebrating their twenty-first birthday at several clubs in Honolulu when Fireball offered them a ride home to Kailua. All three were intoxicated—well over the legal limit. Fireball was double over.

I pull off at the next scenic lookout—a lesser version of the dramatic Pali Lookout above—after the big bend in the road about a quarter mile below the tunnels. I walk toward a trailhead that will lead me down to the scene of the crash. I'm hiking this steep trail because the twins' father is suing the clubs that served his daughters and the driver. I'm working for Mr. Lindquist's attorney, a partner in a Bishop Street law firm. Tommy recommended me—another reason I owe him. What the job amounts to—in addition to searching the crash site and the vehicle—is investigating each club the doomed threesome went to that night and then interviewing the employees and tracking down other patrons who were there.

This sad job—I know because I've done it before—is complicated by two things: First, club owners don't want their employees to go on record with anyone except their own attorney, who would be defending the clubs in court. Second, ferreting out club goers after the fact can consume more client dollars than the resulting information is worth. Sometimes you get lucky. One witness may clinch the case. Question is: which one?

Despite these challenges, I took this case, and others before it, because too often drunken and/or stoned racer-boys like Fireball—hell bent on killing themselves—take innocents like the Lindquists with them. It makes me angry. And heartsick. These cases, for me, tend to become more like missions. I can't bring back the dead. But I can try to give their grieving families and friends the satisfaction, if not the consolation, of knowing exactly what happened and why.

I'm just starting to look into this particular accident. And the Bishop Street attorney who hired me is in a hurry. The only reason, besides a favor to Tommy, I will go to the Volcano House tomorrow is that I'm waiting on a few things. My HPD friend Creighton Lee says he can get me access to the impound lot to examine the wrecked Honda. But that won't happen until later in the week. And another contact, through Tommy, says he can provide liquor commission reports on the clubs where Fireball and the twins did their drinking. The reports could help determine the history of over-serving in those clubs and whether or not any claims have been made or any litigation filed. But I have to wait for the reports.

From the trailhead I hike steeply downhill toward where Fireball's Honda landed after its dive from the highway above. The terrain is rugged and the underbrush thick. It's slow going. The picture emerging of the accident is pretty much what I expected from the facts of the case.

A dozen or so friends had been drinking at the clubs. Neither girl knew Fireball. He was a friend of a friend whom they met at the last club. They hitched a ride home with him when their pal Ashley, who had driven them to the celebration, left earlier than they did to catch a redeye to Denver. Ashley hasn't returned my calls. But that's another story.

Leaving the last club, the Lollipop Lounge, the three climbed into Fireball's Honda and headed up the Pali Highway. His Honda was tricked out with lowered suspension, after-market turbo, nitrous oxide kit, and one of those angry-bee mufflers. *Fast & Furious*. Fireball had accumulated a raft of citations, arrests, and DUIs. His license had been revoked recently for driving 110 mph. On the Kailua-bound ascent, which was slick from a passing shower, Fireball no doubt mashed the gas pedal to the floor. The twins must have been terrified—if they weren't already knocked out from all the alcohol they'd consumed.

When his car screamed into the first tunnel, Fireball was already in trouble. He wasn't as good a driver as he thought. Especially drunk. The Honda's four tires, those essential points of contact with Mother Earth, lost traction on the slick pavement. The car started to slide. Impact marks entering the first tunnel suggest that the Honda's driver's side fender, doors, and rear quarter hit hard as the car began to swerve. It probably entered the second tunnel half-sideways, passenger side of the vehicle leading the way, and failed to negotiate the acute right curve immediately following that tunnel. The Honda collided with the low concrete barrier that separates the two elevated sections of the highway, flipped, and disappeared. An astonished motorist in the town-bound lanes saw the car vanish.

I hug the *pali* and carefully measure my steps. The trail continues steep and slow. But I finally reach the accident site. The impact of the falling car has crushed dwarf *kiawe* and caused a minor landslide. Debris from the wreckage is scattered. There's not much left, just bits and pieces. I scour the scene. I'm looking for physical evidence—receipts, bottles, personal items, and vehicle parts—anything that might corroborate that the three accident victims were sold drinks while intoxicated.

I find several jagged pieces from the car and broken glass on the dark-stained earth. No receipts or bottles. But there is something.

Off in the brush to the side of the debris a small object gleams gold. I step toward the gleam, reach in, and extract a Hawaiian bracelet. It's bent, but not mangled. And it's engraved. *A woman's name?* Apparently not Heather or Lindsay. Odd. Why would the twins, or Fireball, carry another woman's bracelet in the car?

The letters on the bracelet are ornate and difficult to read. Turning it to the light, I think I have the name. The twins' friend who drove them to the party and then flew to Denver. The same friend who hasn't returned my calls. *Ashley.*

five

Sunday morning I'm snoozing when my phone rings. I check my watch. It's not even seven. *Maile?*

I look at the phone. No such luck. Why do I keep hoping?

Caller ID says: RANSOM.

I pick up.

"Hello, Kai?" says the now familiar feminine voice. "It's Donnie. I hope it's not too early."

"No worries," I say. "I had to wake up anyway."

"Oh." She seems ever so slightly taken aback.

"What can I do for you?" I ask.

"I just wanted to fill you in about the arrangements for Monday morning," she says. "You have an e-ticket on Hawaiian Airlines from Honolulu to Hilo, departing at nine-forty. Rex and I will be on the same flight—in first class. Your seat is in the back of the coach cabin. That way, Rex won't suspect you're following us."

"Makes sense," I say.

"At the Hilo Airport Rex and I will be picked up by a chauffeured limo. I've reserved a rental car for you. You can follow us to Volcano House at a discreet distance."

"Your limo will have a head start," I say. "It'll take me a while to pick up the rental car."

"That's okay," she says. "I'm not concerned about Rex's safety on the drive to the hotel. Just once we're there. We'll be staying in a crater-view room on the first floor in the main building. You'll be in a second-floor crater view room in the adjacent building, not far away, but far enough that we won't run into you every time we go out in the hall. I'll stay in touch with you when I can by cell phone."

"Got it." I'm still wondering why she called me at this hour on a Sunday morning.

"Now let's go over the instructions," she says. "You're going to follow Rex, but he's not to know. You'll stay with us—at a distance—everywhere we go. You'll eat in the hotel dining room when we eat, but not at our table. You'll act like any other hotel guest. You and I won't talk when Rex is around. Understood?"

"Yes," I say, not much liking her tone.

"I'll be in touch when I can to let you know my husband's comings and goings."

"Okay," I manage.

"You don't sound too concerned," she says. "This is really important. My husband's life is at stake."

"I am concerned. But it's early and—"

"This was the only time I could call when he wouldn't overhear me," she interrupts. "He's in the shower now. When he's out we'll be together all day."

"Don't worry," I say. "I'll stick with your husband. I won't let him out of my sight."

"Aloha." She hangs up.

No chance of sleep now. I grab a bowl of cereal and flip open my laptop. As I'm spooning in my breakfast I begin a quick and dirty investigation of Rex Ransom. Google provides lots of hits.

What I'm looking for are potential threats to the man I've been hired to protect. Donnie Ransom has already briefed me thoroughly about Pele. Whatevahs. Realistically, I'm concerned more about mortal enemies. Some of what I see brings back memories from two decades ago. Some is new to me.

There's a lot about the protests against the former CEO of Ransom Geothermal, a Montana-based corporation that spearheaded a controversial drilling in the Wao Kele O Puna rainforest. The Save Pele Coalition—the native Hawaiian group that protested the project from the get-go—claimed it violated a state land trust that set aside the pristine rainforest for preservation and for their use and gathering rights. They alleged that this last existing lowland rainforest had been illegally swapped for comparatively barren and worthless land many miles away. And that drilling in their goddess Pele's domain was, to them, tantamount to rape. These were highly charged issues involving the Hawaiians' land, cultural practices, and religion. Before the age of the internet, the protests splashed the headlines and made the radio and TV news.

Ransom received threats. The one act of violence against him came at the hands of SPC radical Ikaika "Sonny Boy" Chang who dragged the CEO from his car into the red mud road Ransom's crew had cut into the forest. Sonny Boy was arrested and denounced by the SPC, since it advocated nonviolence. He did time for the attack, was released, and then arrested again for violating parole. Over the last two decades he'd been in and out jail. Currently it appears he's out. That could be trouble.

Ransom's geothermal operation ultimately failed to produce enough electricity to be commercially viable. He bailed out and the disputed land was ultimately returned to a trust for the benefit of Hawaiians, after years of continued protests and legal wrangling. When the CEO walked away, his former partner Mick London went bankrupt, sued Ransom, but did not prevail in court. London apparently lost everything, including his home. After the court battle, it appears the two men never reconciled. If London still lives on the Big Island, which seems to be the case, he might attend the funeral of a former Ransom company officer. That could also be trouble.

At the same time Ransom pulled out of Puna and was being sued by his former partner, the CEO was going through an ugly divorce from his first wife, Kathryn Bates Ransom—while former beauty queen Donnie Lam waited in the wings. During their bitter divorce, Kathryn, who apparently still resides in the family home in Kona, was questioned by Big Island police about a knife wound to her husband's hand that was treated at Hilo Medical Center. Ransom claimed the wound came from a cooking accident. Those who knew the couple thought otherwise. Kathryn had finally snapped, one neighbor said, and given her cheating husband what he deserved.

It wouldn't surprise me if Rex's ex showed up at the funeral too. Kathryn no doubt knew the family of the deceased and might want to pay her respects. More trouble?

I close my laptop. Three potential threats to my charge over breakfast are three too many. And they only confirm my suspicion that Pele should be the least of Donnie Ransom's worries.

six

Monday morning I show up at the interisland terminal more than the required hour before the nine-forty flight to Hilo. When I check in, there's no sign of Donnie Ransom and her husband. I'm a seasoned island hopper, so I know enough not to check a bag. Especially if I have to pay for the privilege.

I get my carry-on and myself through security, go to the gate, and take an inconspicuous seat in the waiting area. It's early. Only half a dozen passengers have beat me here. I glance at my boarding pass. Seat 26E, at the back of the Boeing 717, as far from first class as you can go. Donnie wasn't kidding. She's put a lot of seats between her husband and me. The Ransoms are probably in row one. I know her type. First class isn't enough. She must be in the first row of first class.

Minutes pass and the boarding area fills. Still no Ransoms. Then I hear the preliminary boarding announcement. The usual stuff. First, families with small children and those who need assistance. Then, first class and elite high-mileage fliers board. And finally the likes of me and everyone else. *Steerage class.*

Where are Donnie and Rex Ransom? Their cabin is about to board.

Then comes another announcement: *Ladies and Gentlemen, at this time we welcome aboard our first class passengers.*

Still no sign of the Ransoms. Then it dawns on me. They're probably in the elite fliers' lounge with other well-heeled passengers. They should emerge now that their cabin has been called.

Sure enough. First Donnie appears. Then, behind her, an old man. He bears faint resemblance to the robust Rex Ransom in the media two decades earlier. The contrast between those images and his present self couldn't be more pronounced. Or the contrast between his bent profile and the erect form of his younger wife.

Rex Ransom in his heyday—ice-blue eyes, raven hair, prominent jaw, barrel chest, massive arms, and aggressive, in-your-face posture—is all but gone. In his place is a pale-eyed, silver haired, bent and frail septuagenarian who walks with a cane and looks not ahead, but down at his unsure footsteps. A lifelong smoker who recently suffered a heart attack, has he finally kicked the habit? Whatevahs. The damage has obviously been done.

Time has ravaged the once powerful CEO more than his foes ever did. I can see no reason why anyone, even his worst enemy, even Pele herself, would want to punish him further. The years have taken their toll. The transformation would sadden me more if I hadn't just been refreshing my memory about what he did at Wao Kele O Puna.

I watch Donnie Ransom take her husband's arm, the one not holding the cane, and lead him down the jetway. The age difference between them glares. To the casual onlooker Donnie must appear to be a faithful daughter assisting her aged father. The fact that Donnie looks local and Rex is obviously a mainlander doesn't alter the impression. I wonder about their relationship as husband and wife. Twenty years ago when they met, he was a CEO in his mid-fifties accustomed to calling the shots. She was barely thirty and a beauty. He had money; she had youth. Now he's so clearly dependent on her that their roles have obviously changed.

They disappear down the jetway. Minutes later, after most passengers have boarded, my turn finally comes. I lug my carry-on down the jetway and onto the airplane.

I was right. The Ransoms are sitting in row one in plush royal purple lounge chairs. I try not to make eye contact with them, but I'm stopped by traffic in the first class cabin. Rex Ransom turns toward me and before I can avert my glance we make eye contact. He smiles. His smile is warm and disarming. I'm surprised. I find myself being drawn to him and smile back.

Then I walk on slowly down the aisle, kicking myself for this slip. I'm off to a bad start being incognito. Donnie, who's buried in an airline magazine, has fortunately missed the encounter.

I pass between the purple curtains that separate the first class and coach cabins and work my way to the back of the airplane. 26E is not only in the very last row, but also in the middle of three seats. I wedge in.

The airplane finally gets pushed back from the gate, taxies to the runway, and takes off over Keʻehi Lagoon. The engines howl. I look straight ahead at the purple seatback in front of me. It says: "Life vest under your seat." That's probably more reassuring to passengers who are in the ocean less than I am.

The Boeing soars by the skyline of Waikīkī and I glance out the window. Vog. The brown haze is still drifting up to

O'ahu from the ongoing eruption. Hilo Airport and the roads
to and within Hawai'i Volcanoes National Park will be choked
with onlookers. I wonder how the potential crowds may affect
my keeping tabs on Ransom.

Time slips by. Moloka'i, Lāna'i, and Maui pass under our
wings. No sooner do I down the passion-guava nectar a flight
attendant offers me than the Big Island comes into view.

Snow-capped Mauna Kea towers above the clouds. This
tallest mountain in Hawai'i—tallest in the world measured
from the sea floor—evokes memories for me no doubt different from those of most who fly by this looming giant.

My parents died here. I was eight. After their plane crash
I was *hanaied* by my auntie's *ohana* on O'ahu's North Shore and
then sent to an uncle in California to attend prep school. Later
I toted my surfboard to college at Point Loma. How I ended
up in the army after my freshman year and eventually made it
back to the islands is a story longer than this Honolulu to Hilo
flight. Laydahs.

The airplane descends along the emerald-green Hamakua
coast and lapping waves that shimmer in the morning sun. The
liner banks steeply and then touches down in Hilo—delivering
me to my strange gig.

The cabin door opens and I see the Ransoms stepping off
the airplane. Five minutes later I finally wrench myself from
my seat and navigate the narrow aisle. I'm almost the last passenger off. No Ransoms in sight.

I catch up with them as they're leaving Baggage Claim, follow them from the terminal to the curb, and watch them climb
into a black Lincoln. He gets in first. Before she follows him,

she turns, sees me, and nods—discreetly, of course. Then the door closes and they're gone.

The air is thick with vog—formerly rare in Hilo—and the airport thick with people. Word has gotten out about the eruption. I walk to the car rental agencies located in the tin-roofed longhouse across from Baggage Claim. Directly behind is the lot that's usually full of cars. Not today.

I step to the agency whose contract I hold and take my place in a line of a half dozen customers. I wait a minute or two. Nobody's moving and nobody's driving away in a car.

Finally the first customer in line waves his contract angrily and stalks away muttering. The next screams that he and his wife have flown from Canada for a Hawai'i vacation planned for years. But where's their rental car? More customers walk away, instead of driving away.

By the time I reach the desk I know the score. There's been a run on rental cars because of the eruption. A contract means nothing.

"I'm not just going *holoholo*." I tell the agent, which means something like to go on holiday. "I've got a job to do. I need some wheels."

"See those three cars over there?" She points across the lot to a red Ferrari, a black Maserati, and a bright yellow Porsche Boxster. "Those are our exotics—the only cars available."

My contract is for a subcompact, not an exotic. So I ask: "How much?"

She explains that I can rent the Ferrari for five bills a day, the Maserati for four and a quarter, or the Boxster for three and a half. I have no idea if Donnie will pay, but I hear myself saying, "I'll take the Porsche."

I sign the papers, grab the key, and slip into the yellow roadster. Twenty-three miles on the clock. Brand new. I put down the top and head for Volcano. This is hardly the kind of car to tail someone. *I hope she pays.*

I take the airport service road from the rental lot and turn left onto the Māmalahoa Highway, more familiarly known as Hawai'i Belt Road. Then I cruise the outskirts of Hilo town, savoring the whine of the flat six motor behind me. *How the other half lives. Or is it the 1%?* There's little chance I can catch the Ransoms' limo, but I can have fun trying. Too bad the Porsche is an automatic. Sports cars are for shifting.

Not too long ago this part of Hilo was sparsely populated, but now I find myself passing Toyota and Honda dealers, Walgreens, Macy's, Pizza Hut, and Jack in the Box. The national chains are sprouting like poisonous mushrooms in the lush soil of this island. Inspired by the lure of tropical paradise, tourists come from thousands of miles to eat fast food and shop in big-box stores, just like at home. Go figgah.

The road begins to climb. The scent of ginger fills the air.

I leave Hilo and its strip malls behind. The Hawai'i Belt Road circles the entire island, but I'm only taking the thirty-mile portion that rises four thousand feet to Volcano. My quibble about the Boxster's automatic transmission disappears when I feel how quickly and seamlessly it shifts. The Porsche purrs into the greener and cooler stretch of highway.

By the village of Kea'au I pass the turnoff for Kalapana, once famous for its black sand beach. That beach, a victim of flows from the East Rift Zone, is now buried under tons of lava. *Pele at work.*

Moving into the goddess's domain, where the evidence of seemingly supernatural power shows all around in the very earth, sea, and sky, sparks a weird thought: What if Donnie's right—I still can't wrap my head around it—and Pele actually *is* out to get her husband? I remind myself that I agreed to this madness for one reason—and one reason only. I owe Tommy.

I concentrate on the road ahead and try to catch the Ransoms. It's a short road. And things could be worse. I could be driving a subcompact instead of this rocket.

So I push the pedal and the Porsche instantly responds. The roadside becomes a blur of farms and forests and macadamia orchards. Ginger and lavender grow wild on the shoulder. The hamlets of Kurtistown, Mountain View, and Glenwood barely interrupt the countryside. Altitude markers count the climb: 2,500 feet . . . 3,000 feet . . . 3,500 feet. The air streaming through the roadster grows cooler.

When the scenery changes from lush green to the grey-bitten of higher altitude, I catch the black Lincoln and hang back. We pass the village of Volcano. And just beyond it comes the entrance to Hawai'i Volcanoes National Park.

The limo turns left and stops at the ranger station. I pull off to the side of the highway and put up the top. I don't want to sit directly behind the Lincoln while the driver pays admission. When the limo moves on, I pull up, pay, and swing into the Volcano House, barely a stone's throw away. The Lincoln parks under the portico and the Ransoms climb out.

I keep my distance.

Beside the limo sits a white Ford Expedition with emergency lights on top and PARK RANGER emblazoned on the side. Did Ransom have an official escort? The Ranger himself is nowhere in sight.

After the old man crawls from the limo he steadies himself with his cane and his wife takes his free arm. Once they disappear inside the hotel and the limo drives away, I park at the far end of the nearly full lot, as much out of sight as I can get the yellow Porsche.

When I climb from the car, the odor of sulfur hanging in the cool air hits me like a wall. Fumes from the volcanoes can be hazardous, especially for the elderly.

Bad idea to bring him. But his own, according to his wife.

seven

If you've never been here, the barn-red clapboard façade of the Volcano House resembles, well, a barn. Don't let the hotel's plain and unadorned exterior fool you into thinking that inside, by contrast, is a luxury resort. What you see is pretty much what you get. But you don't come here for luxury. You come for the view. This is the only hotel I know of, at least in this part of the world, that's perched on the rim of an active volcano.

I step into the Volcano House and recall from previous visits that a hotel by this name dates back to an 1846 grass hut and a later wooden structure containing the famous fireplace whose enduring flames are immortalized in *Ripley's Believe it or Not*. The hotel expanded in 1891 and remained in operation well into the twentieth century, until it burned to the ground in 1940. Legend has it that the fireplace's celebrated flame kept going even after the hotel burned. Embers were rescued from the ruin and returned to the hearth when the hotel reopened. That's why the management says, "Volcano House, where the fire and aloha spirit never go out!"

I navigate a huddle of guests in the lobby admiring those perpetual flames, and head to the registration desk. A Park Service sign there confirms my fears about the poisonous air around the volcanoes.

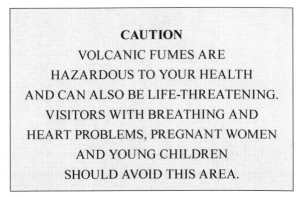

CAUTION
VOLCANIC FUMES ARE
HAZARDOUS TO YOUR HEALTH
AND CAN ALSO BE LIFE-THREATENING.
VISITORS WITH BREATHING AND
HEART PROBLEMS, PREGNANT WOMEN
AND YOUNG CHILDREN
SHOULD AVOID THIS AREA.

The Kīlauea Caldera is bulging. The Halemaʻumaʻu Crater, Pele's traditional home, is a lake of fire. Steam vents along the Crater Rim Trail are spewing noxious gas. And, of course, the East Rift Zone continues to erupt. But nobody seems concerned. Because that's why they're here. To experience it all.

There's a line at the registration desk. I take my place at the end and look around. Things haven't changed much here since my last visit. Behind the veneer desk are cubbyholes for room keys and guests' mail, an ancient phone with three dozen buttons for the various rooms, an adding machine with a paper roll, and a yellowed keyboard and monitor that look like they've been around since the dawn of the personal computer. Plaques on a nearby wall, dating back a few years, attest to the hotel restaurant's culinary excellence.

The guest at the front of the line rings the bell—one of those old-fashioned chrome thingies with a clapper on top.

A *mu'umu'u*-clad woman appears and begins to assist. She's the essence of Hawaiian hospitality. Warm smile. Soft voice. Genuine *aloha*. How a people whose land, government, and culture were stolen from them can be so pleasant to the heirs of the thieves is a miracle to me. I guess that tourist cliché about warm-hearted, generous Hawaiians has a nugget of truth.

The receptionist's job isn't easy. Apparently some in line don't have reservations. She has the unenviable task of informing them that the hotel is full. I'm glad my room has been booked in advance by my client. That's what she tells me, anyway. And I hope the hotel doesn't give away my room like the rental agency gave away my car. The desk clerk calmly and courteously explains the situation to those without reservations. One by one they step away, crestfallen.

"So sorry," she says. *"Mahalo* for understanding." Her gentle voice sounds vaguely familiar.

When my turn comes she looks me up and down, smiles warmly, and says, "Kai, long time no see!"

"Shoots," I respond, recalling her face now. But not her name.

"You remembah me, yeah? Pualani." She shifts to Pidgin. "I wuz working hea when you come 'bout your parents."

"I remembah," I say. More than a decade ago I came to the Big Island to investigate their airplane crash. I was a *keiki* when it happened. So by the time I returned in my late twenties the trail was cold. But it was something I had to do. I didn't find much, but afterwards I spent a few nights at the Volcano House to unwind. That's when I met Pualani. She was sympathetic to the tale of my orphaning, which her warm friendliness coaxed from me. One evening after her shift we strolled the Crater

Rim Trail under the stars. We talked-story. I liked her but never saw her again. Until now.

"Same job still," she says. "But I get one teenager. Imagine dat!"

"Nah," I say. "You stay so young." She's filled out a little since then and her still pretty face shows the passage of time.

"You get *keiki*, Kai?" she asks. "You marry?"

"Nah." I shake my head. "Working too much."

"So why you hea? Anoddah investigation?"

"Holoholo," I say. I can't tell her why I'm really at the Volcano House. "Can fin' my reservation?"

"Shoots." She types on her ancient keypad and peers at the yellowed monitor. "Mr. Kai Cooke—fo' two nights. Lucky you get one reservation. We bin sold out. Turn lots of custom-ahs away. Dey all come to see da eruption. Pele at work again!"

"She da boss ovah hea," I joke. "Don't mess wit' Pele."

"Fo' sure," she says. "I afraid fo' one hotel guest—afraid Pele gonna get 'em. He check in awready. He old man now, bent n' walk wit' one cane. But I rec'onize 'em. He da guy dat drill in Pele's rainforest. She gonna get 'em."

"You really t'ink so?" I didn't expect that time-ravaged Rex Ransom would be so easily recognized.

She nods. "He come for da funeral," Pualani says. "But he bettah watch out or his own funeral gonna come bumbye—jus' like da oddah two."

"So you t'ink Pele *make* da oddahs?" I wonder if she's pulling my leg. "And she gonna *make* dis old guy too?"

Pualani gives me a room key, a map of the hotel, and a wink—a wink that seems as mysterious as the goddess herself.

"T'anks, eh?"

I step away from the desk and glance at the map. About half of the rooms in the hotel have crater views, some in the main building, some in an adjacent addition. I did my homework, so I know that Donnie and her husband are staying in the main building on the first floor in room one, the largest crater-view room. My room also overlooks the crater but, as Donnie explained on the phone, is in the addition on the second floor at the other end of the hotel. Close enough to watch over Ransom, but far enough to keep out of his sight.

I walk from the registration desk through the main building to the addition. On the way I pass the Ransoms' room. The door is slightly ajar. I hear voices. I stand against the opposite wall out of view and listen. Donnie is talking to her husband.

"What about me?" Her voice rises in irritation. "I'm your wife!"

"You have nothing to worry about," Rex Ransom replies.

"That's easy for you to say!" she shouts.

The door bursts open. Donnie stalks out. I start walking again toward my room.

"*Kai?*"

I hear my name called in a stage whisper and turn around.

Donnie closes the door and steps gracefully toward me, her lustrous black hair shimmering even in the dim hallway. "Did you check in?" Her tone sweetens. She smiles.

"Yes, just now," I say. "Howzit going?"

"Fine," she says, her red lipstick punctuating her smile. "We're having a wonderful time—never mind my worries about Rex."

I let that one pass. "Did Mr. Ransom see me on the airplane?" I know the answer, but at this awkward moment I can think of nothing else to say.

"I doubt it," Donnie says. "Even if he did, to my husband you'd be just another coach passenger hiking to the back of the airplane."

"That's good, I guess," I say. "I better go—in case he comes looking for you."

"Oh, I don't think we have to worry about that." Her mascaraed eyes sparkle.

"Aloha—for now." I start walking.

"I'll be in touch, Kai," she says and moments later the door to the Ransoms' room snaps shut.

I walk the passageway to the addition, hike the stairs to the second floor, and step to the end of the hall. The door to room thirty-three opens with my key to a flowered carpet, Hawaiian quilt on a double bed, small bath, and a *koa* desk and rocker. That's about it. No TV. No WĪFi. No minibar. But there's something better: serenity.

The room has good vibes—and two windows overlooking the crater. I open them. Cool air wafts in—expected at four thousand feet—and that omnipresent smell of sulfur. I gaze down on Kīlauea Caldera, the collapsed but still active volcano nearly three miles long. Fifteen Aloha Stadiums, they say, could fit inside. Smoke twirls up from vents in the charred and cracked floor. The mottled surface resembles the scorched remains of a wildfire.

Far in the distance at the southern end of the caldera gapes the half-mile wide Halemaʻumaʻu Crater. The view from the hotel of the fire goddess's home is obscured by spiraling smoke. Yet the crater looks majestic, haunting, and huge. *Pele.*

The air suddenly feels cooler and I get chicken skin.

I leave my bag in the room, shut the windows, and head downstairs to the hotel's famous fireplace. I walk past the Ransoms' room again. Their door is closed now, but I can still hear voices. Can't make out words, but I can hear tone. It's the tone of a couple disagreeing. Though there's no screaming, I find myself wondering about the picture of devotion I saw earlier at Honolulu Airport.

A brusque word now and then, a crisp exchange, might not be all that unusual in a marriage—especially if one spouse persists in doing something the other believes is dangerous. Donnie Ransom fears for her husband's life at the Volcano House. He insists on coming anyway. Wouldn't she be upset? Wouldn't she feel ignored, hurt, and angry? Wouldn't she naturally speak out? Not to mention that she's a bit haughty anyway.

I walk on. What do I know? I'm just a guy who has a lot to learn about women. Otherwise, Maile would return my calls.

I head for the fire. The Ransoms obviously don't need my services at this moment. Especially as a marriage counselor.

eight

At the registration desk I see the olive trousers, khaki shirt, and smoky-the-bear hat of a park ranger. I remember the white Expedition in the hotel's lot and wonder again if he's here because of Rex Ransom. The ranger turns from the desk and walks toward me. His brass nametag says DOUGLAS CRISP.

"Aloha, Ranger Crisp," I say, hoping to test my theory. "What brings you to the Volcano House?"

"Escaped mental patient," the ranger says. "She may be hiding in the park. I just left a BOLO at the front desk."

"Be on the lookout?"

"Right," he says. "We're warning hotel guests. She's a grey-haired old woman who wanders around half naked. She appears harmless, but she's unstable and should be considered dangerous. Her name is Serena Barrymore."

"Serena Barrymore?" I repeat. "Sounds made-up."

"It may be," Ranger Crisp says. "Another name she uses is Goddess Hi'iaka. Hi'iaka, in Hawaiian myth, is Pele's youngest and favorite sister—keeper and protector of the rainforest and flowering 'ōhi'a tree. Barrymore took that identification to the extreme and actually killed a man for chopping down one of those trees."

"You're kidding."

"I wish I was," the ranger says. "Barrymore shoved him into the path of a Hilo bus. When she was apprehended she claimed to be above human law. Her victim was in a coma for months until his family decided to remove life support. Barrymore was indicted for second-degree murder. She never stood trial, though. She was evaluated and deemed unfit."

"Sad case," I say.

"Back when they were drilling Wao Kele O Puna she threatened people involved in the project. We've increased our presence in the park because Stan Nagahara's funeral tomorrow will bring back some of those same people. She might target them."

"I'll keep my eyes open." I head for the fireplace.

I'm right. The ranger is concerned about Rex Ransom. I add another potential threat to my list—this one embodying the all-too-real impact of the legendary goddess—as I walk to the Volcano House's famous fireplace.

The *koa*-paneled room where the celebrated embers glow looks like the lobby of an Old West inn. Two saddle-leather sofas and a log table between them sit on a wine-colored carpet. The room is dim except for those eternal flames and sconce lights on the paneled walls. Two *koa* rockers flank the hearth. One is already occupied by an aloha-shirted local man rocking slowly like he's in no hurry. I take the other and say, "Howzit?"

"'Kay, brah." He smiles.

I smile back and gaze at the fire. Those hundred-year-old flames lick up the chimney and radiate warmth into the room, taking the chill out of my bones. I move closer to the fire. Above the mantel a likeness of Pele herself, carved in bronze-hued lava rock, peers down on me imperiously. No soft, gauzy, delicate angel, this woman. She's a broad-featured, large-breasted, tough-love goddess whose huge hands reach out to either side of the mantel, embracing and dominating the flames. Here's another reminder of her power.

"Das Pele," says my fellow rocker who sees me gazing at her. "She da queen, brah."

"She da real t'ing," I reply.

"You like study her, or somet'ing? Serious kine?"

"Nah, jus' looking."

"Sure, brah," my companion says. "Me, I jus' waiting. Limo drivah, you know. Deliver my passengers awready. Jus' waiting fo' drive 'em aroun.'"

"Who dey?" I ask.

"Not suppose to say, brah."

I suddenly realize why he's not saying. "Black limo? You drive from da Hilo airport one hour ago? One couple in da car?"

"Yeah. How'd you know, brah?"

"I recognize 'em. Dey famous, eh?"

"Not famous anymo'. I know 'em back when. Da wahine wuz one beauty queen, brah. And she still look pretty good! And da guy, he wuz da geothermal king."

"You mean da guy dat drill on Pele's lan'?" I want to keep him talking.

"Yeah, brah," he says. "Lots of people dey talk stink 'bout him, but he always treat me good. Da protestahs dat fight geothermal bin all *pakalolo* growers. Dey no like him drilling in dere *pakalolo* patch. Das all."

"Really, brah?"

"Is true," he says. "One protestah get jail time fo' *pakalolo* and firearms."

"Whatevahs," I say.

"You no hear 'bout dat?" he continues. "Da geothermal king jus' follow da example of King David Kalākaua. Da King talk wit' da guy Thomas Edison, dat invent electricity, 'bout making power from da Kīlauea Volcano. Dat was mo' den one hundred years ago, brah! "

"Fo' sure? Kalākaua and Thomas Edison?" It sounds improbable.

"Is one fact of history," he says. "Happen in 1881." He keeps talking. "Geothermal not all bad. Get da power outta da groun', brah, so we nevah depend on foreign oil. Plus da geothermal king make jobs for da people."

"You know 'em long time?"

"Yeah, brah. Maybe twenty years. Use to drive 'em when he da boss. Know his firs' wife too. But dey divorce now. Ho! She hūhū. Really hate 'em, brah. Try stab 'em once."

"Da firs' wife? She stab 'em?" I recall Googling the same information. Small world.

He nods. "Mr. Ransom nevah press charges. No like his wife fo' go to jail—even though they getting one divorce."

"Da ex-wife here for da funeral?"

"Dunno, brah," he says. "I no drive her anymo'."

"I'm Kai." I offer my hand. "Maybe buy you one drink sometime?"

"Shoots," he says and we shake local-style. "Cannot drink on da job."

"Maybe latah?"

He nods. "I'm Kawika."

"Aloha, Kawika." I rise from my rocker and leave behind the everlasting flames. And the everlasting gaze of Pele.

nine

I pass the Ransoms' room again and this time nothing's shakin'. Door closed. No voices. I cross to the addition, climb the stairs to my room, and check the phone. No messages. My cell isn't ringing either. All I can do is wait.

I'm not what you'd call a patient person. Since there's no TV in the room, I crack a glossy book on the desk about Hawai'i Volcanoes National Park and flop on the bed. I fluff the pillow behind my head and gaze at the full-color plates of craters, caverns, fissures and vents. It feels good to get horizontal after the flight to Hilo, the drive to Volcano, and the busywork of checking in and getting settled. The park, the book says, was established in 1916 and includes more than five hundred square miles of land and two active volcanoes, Mauna Loa, the world's most massive, and Kīlauea, one of the world's most active. Little wonder Pele has such a lively following, since her volcano just keeps on keeping on.

My cell phone rings. RANSOM.

"Kai," Donnie says in a whisper when I answer, "we're going to walk the Crater Rim Trail to The Steaming Bluff."

"Steaming Bluff?" I say. "Did you see the warning at the hotel desk?" A picture of the almost mystical steam vents comes to mind: wisps of vapor floating up from dozens of openings in the lava rock and hovering over the trail. Eerily beautiful. But the super-heated underground water that rises in misty beauty can carry potentially lethal fumes, such as the Park Service sign warned about. Fumes that may make breathing difficult for even the most robust tourist.

"There's no stopping Rex," she says. "If there were, we wouldn't be here. And you wouldn't either."

"Okay, I'll follow you."

I hop off the bed, head downstairs, and step outside onto the Crater Rim Trail, where it passes in front of the Volcano House. I move around the corner of the hotel and wait for the Ransoms to show.

Five minutes pass, and finally they come hand-in-hand, working their way across the lawn to the trail. She's steadying him as they step onto the path. Rex Ransom looks no more healthy than he did on the airplane. He's bent and his eyes point down. He hobbles along, a cane in the hand that isn't held by his wife. Stroll is too elegant a word for how they walk. It's more like a crawl. But the picture of the two together looks like devotion, despite the harsh tones coming from their room earlier.

The Ransoms head in the westerly direction, toward the steam vents and Halemaʻumaʻu Crater. The trail by the hotel is more like a sidewalk, asphalt and a yard wide. A lava rock retaining wall, about waist high, stands between the cliff and the Kīlauea Caldera, hundreds of feet below. It's late afternoon and the smell of sulfur hangs in the cool air. Aside from the sulfur, I can spot no immediate threat to the former geothermal king. I give the Ransoms a minute to clear the hotel before I come out of hiding.

Just as I emerge, a middle-aged man also steps from the hotel and onto the trail. He's got a touch of grey in his sideburns and is talking on his cell phone. He shuts the phone and heads in the same direction as the Ransoms.

This is good. If the man stays on the trail between them and me, he will provide concealment. But the more I consider this, the less likely it seems. The man looks fit and should easily overtake the toddling couple. I follow him, not expecting to see him for long.

Ahead of both of us, the Ransoms are barely moving.

To my surprise the man with a touch of grey travels as slowly as they do. And it's not because he's stopping at every turn to gawk at the caldera below. He's just ambling along, eyes ahead, keeping pace with the Ransoms. I maintain the same pace, at a distance. The trail loses the asphalt and the lava rock wall upon leaving the Volcano House and turns to gravel, bordered by tree ferns. The caldera side of the trail sprouts guardrails. The tree ferns called *hapu'u* climb high overhead like giant green umbrellas. They look primitive and Jurassic. I might expect a dinosaur as much as a human assailant to jump out around the next bend.

The air warms as we approach the steam vents and smells increasingly like rotten eggs. The sun tries to burn through the sulfur-infused vapor, but manages only a pale wafer in the sky.

Ahead on the misty trail I can barely make out the red blooms of the native flowering *'ōhi'a,* the tree that mad woman Serena Barrymore, a.k.a. Goddess Hi'iaka killed for. As I get closer I see a bird hovering above the *'ōhi'a,* whose breast and head are also red—the Hawaiian honeycreeper called *'Apapane.*

The man with a touch of grey isn't noticing the tree or the bird. He's watching the Ransoms. I'm thinking this is no coincidence. I know what to look for. And this guy is a professional. Or an amateur masquerading as a professional. Is this another foe to add to my list?

The man keeps pace with the Ransoms. He walks by the pale-yellow and red berries of the 'ōhelo plant—a traditional favorite of Pele—growing about waist high on the side of the trail. He doesn't seem to notice the berries. It's a little early in March to harvest the 'ōhelo, but already the plants have clusters about the size of blueberries. Donnie Ransom could pick the berries and offer them to the goddess, if my client truly believes Pele plans revenge on her husband. A ritual offering thrown into the fire pit might just do the trick. Or at least make Donnie feel better.

But the Ransoms walk by the 'ōhelo. And so does the man following them.

The trail keeps meandering, and I keep losing the Ransoms and then picking them up again. At one turn when they stop, the man stops too, and glances back at me. I see him make what appears to be a mental note. Does he think I'm following him? Does he think I'm following the Ransoms? He pulls his cell phone again and makes another call. He's done within twenty seconds. *Strange.*

We all start moving again—the Ransoms, the man between us, and me. The trail twists and turns, emerges from the overgrown jungle, and then weaves along the cliff to The Steaming Bluff.

The Ransoms stop at the first vent along the trail, a gaping hole in the earth the size of a compact car. Steam wafts up thicker than chimney smoke. The fumes can't be good for Ransom, who looks every bit the candidate for another heart attack. The only thing between the former CEO and the smoldering abyss are two slim guardrails on the edge of the trail. But a man of his size could easily slip through them. He leans over the top rail to get a better look. Mrs. Ransom is a half step away from becoming a widow. She scolds him.

Seeing him precariously balanced like that recalls the story of the young park volunteer who tumbled into one of these same vents. She was overcome by scalding vapor and didn't make it out. This happened a few decades ago when Ransom was drilling nearby, and quickly turned into a cautionary tale at this park. So he must have heard about it. I hope he remembers. An elderly man in his condition is no match for a steam vent.

As Rex Ransom gazes into the gaping hole, I stop. The man between us also stops. Then things change quickly.

The vague outline of someone emerges from the mist at the opposite end of the trail. He seems to be wearing a black mask and running towards the Ransoms. He reaches into a pouch at his waistline, pulls a metallic object, and points it in the couple's direction. The thick vapor makes it hard to tell what's happening. He keeps coming.

Alarm bells go off in my head. A Touch of Grey snaps to attention and starts running toward the Ransoms. I break into a run too, staying right behind him. I don't like this guy being between my clients and me.

The masked man keeps coming.

Damn! Already I feel like I've failed. I didn't really believe the old man was in danger here from anything more than old age. Guess I was wrong.

I close in on the Ransoms and so does A Touch of Grey. We're both flying at top speed, evenly spaced. But the masked man beats us to point blank range.

The vapor distorts everything. But this much I can see. Before he reaches the couple and the masked man, A Touch of Grey veers off the trail to the right, away from the scene, and disappears. *Where's he going?* Rex Ransom, still gazing into the vent, doesn't appear to notice him. Or the masked man.

Now I'm almost upon the couple and the approaching man. I halt. The man passes the Ransoms and keeps going—metallic object still in his hand. Now he's heading for me. I'm about to duck off the trail myself, since I'm unarmed. As he approaches me he raises his hand not holding the object. *What's he doing?*

The mist clears enough that I get a better look at him and the object. It has a cord leading to his ears. It's not a gun. It's a digital media player.

The runner passes and I see that his mask is actually a kerchief over his mouth and nose, probably to filter the toxic air. And from his graceful gait and curvaceous figure I'm convinced this man is actually a woman. She moves her hand again. Now I understand. She's waving to me. I wave back.

Maybe the goddess is playing tricks on me?

ten

After following the Ransoms through the hotel's breakfast buffet the next morning—with no sign of A Touch of Grey—I'm in the driver's seat of the yellow Boxster at quarter to nine, ready for the funeral. Ready for anything.

The black Lincoln pulls up to the portico and the waiting couple climbs in. He's in a dark suit and she's in a flowered but also dark *muʻumuʻu*. When the limo passes me and swings onto Crater Rim Drive, I wait about thirty seconds and then fire up the Boxster. The flat six motor roars. Aiming the ragtop in the direction of the limo, I keep my distance so this bright yellow machine isn't a dead giveaway. But I know where we're going. And it's not far.

The Kīlauea Military Camp chapel is less than a mile away, just beyond the Steaming Bluff. Stanley Nagahara, the deceased, was a veteran and a longstanding resident of Volcano, the village just outside the park's entrance. His memorial service will draw neighbors and fellow veterans, as evidenced by the mix of aloha attire and uniforms now climbing from cars and trucks around the chapel. But others, including myself, my client, and her husband, have trekked here because Nagahara had been a corporate attorney who, during the company's heyday, represented Ransom Geothermal to Hawai'i county and state governments, after having worked for the state himself for many years.

I park in an unobtrusive spot in the camp and wait. Across the picturesque rolling lawns are a few dozen cottages that flank a small headquarters and reception building. Behind these, more cottages straddle the meandering tree-lined roads. The camp looks more like a resort than an active base because its main purpose in recent years has been to provide a vacation spot for current and retired military personnel. The chapel resembles a barracks, though, except for a raised section of roof above the entrance resembling a bell tower.

The Lincoln pulls in front of the chapel and the Ransoms climb the steps to its open doors. They file in and other funeralgoers follow. I lock the Boxster and join them.

I stride in wearing my one black aloha shirt—reserved for funerals, weddings, and other somber occasions. I don't know a soul except my client, and I know her only slightly. So I opt not to leave a sympathy card—typically filled with cash to help defray funeral expenses—as the Ransoms do, or walk through the receiving line. But I do go through the motions of signing the guest book, at least, and then try to disappear as the sort of casual acquaintance who shows up at funerals but avoids open caskets and grieving widows. I grab a seat in the back, power off my cell phone, and watch the Ransoms as they approach the casket.

The chapel has a dozen mahogany pews on either side of a carpet runner. Up front there's a portable pulpit and a communion table and, behind those, a royal blue curtain. Grey-green walls reinforce the barracks feel.

I'm ready to get this funeral over. The start time is nine, but the service won't likely begin until family and friends finish paying their respects. And the line is long.

Up front someone speaks his name and Mr. Ransom waves. Even at this distance, I notice a nasty scar in the webbing between his thumb and first finger. I'm contemplating the scar when someone slides into the pew next to me.

"Howzit?" he says. "Remembah me? Kawika, da limo drivah."

"Eh, Kawika," I say. "Howzit?"

"I no expect to see you hea, brah," he replies. "Know da guy?"

"Nah, jus' one frien' of a frien'," I say, hoping he'll let my vagueness slide.

We talk story quietly and time passes. I pump him for information about the Ransoms without seeming to pump. As we're talking A Touch of Grey enters the church and sits across the aisle from us. I don't really like this guy, whoever he is, hanging around my clients. But there's not much I can do about it inside the chapel.

Kawika doesn't notice the man, but turns to watch a tall middle-aged woman in black stride elegantly in and join the line. She stands out. It's not just her black dress. There are plenty inside the chapel. But the way she wears it. And her coiffured hair. She's in a class by herself.

By now Donnie and Rex Ransom have made their way through the receiving line with handshakes and hugs and even a bow, and are finding seats near the front of the chapel. As they pass the statuesque woman, Donnie winces and the old man nods but does not smile. The stately figure that provoked these reactions doesn't move.

"Das da ex." Kawika points to the tall woman. "Das her."

I recall the story about Ransom's ex cutting him with a kitchen knife. And that is some scar on Ransom's hand. Kathryn Ransom doesn't look the type to have carved it there. But I keep watching her. After she works her way through the line, she strides to the back of the church. She stares straight ahead blankly, without turning in her ex-husband's direction, then takes a seat next to A Touch of Grey. They exchange glances. Do they know each other?

A younger version of Ransom's ex, mid-twenties I'd guess, hurries into the chapel. If she's not huffing, she's certainly breathing fast. She slides into the pew that holds the former Mrs. Ransom and sits next to her, on the other side of the mystery man.

The two women in black look like a matched set. Same posture. Same elegant gestures. Same coiffured hair. I ask Kawika and he confirms: Ransom's daughter. And he sounds impressed when he tells me she attended Vassar College.

On the other side of the chapel a bearded, dreadlocked local guy in camouflage wanders in looking lost.

Kawika sees me studying him and says, "Das Sonny Boy." The unlikely figure passes. "Must be outta jail on parole. He da *pakalolo* king."

"Who Sonny Boy?" I ask, surveying his gaunt, tortured face, but I recall even before Kawika speaks. I let him talk.

"Da protestah, brah. Da one dat attack Mr. Ransom. Get nine mont's in prison fo' dat. Sonny Boy wen hate da drillers. Surprise he hea."

"T'ink he jus' come to pay respects?"

"Dunno, brah. Sonny Boy no like da geothermal drilling. He no like Mr. Ransom. Or da oddah guy. Maybe he jus' glad Mr. Nagahara dead. Maybe he wish Mr. Ransom dead too."

When the service finally starts, it's full of platitudes about the deceased: good father, loving husband, loyal servant of the state, respected attorney, etc. But I don't sense much compassion in the church for the man, despite the occasional wet eye in the crowd. A few friends and family members file up to the pulpit to offer a few words about the departed. Nobody says boo about Nagahara's role in the geothermal project in the rainforest, which suggests that most in attendance would rather forget that episode in his life.

Ransom himself sits in the front of the chapel motionless. But once when he turns, I see his face. It shows no grief. It shows nothing. The former CEO appears to have come out of a sense of obligation rather than a feeling of friendship.

As the speakers drone on I find myself feeling blue. A man has died and few who knew him seem deeply moved. When my time comes I'd rather just vanish in a giant wave, without fanfare, than be remembered with such little affection.

A commotion at the back of the chapel makes me turn around. So does Kawika. A man who resembles Father Time, long white beard and all, stumbles down the aisle. He looks for a seat, but no one is making room. As he passes I get a whiff of him. It's barely mid-morning and he smells like he's been knocking 'em back since dawn.

The current purveyor of platitudes at the pulpit tries to ignore the bearded figure, but he's already stolen the show. Finally he finds a seat. Those sitting by him slide this way and that—giving him a wide berth. Ransom turns around, sees the old drunk, and the color drains from the CEO's face. He knows this man. And he's not overjoyed to see him.

"Das Mick," Kawika says. "Mr. Ransom's old partner. Mick—he go broke when Ransom Geothermal pull out. Belly up. Fo' sure."

"Mick London?" I recall his name from my web browsing.

"Das him, brah."

That makes three enemies of the man I've been hired to protect under this one roof—his ex-partner, his ex-wife, and the ex-protester who did jail time for attacking him. Not to mention the operative who seems to follow the CEO every-where. And possibly knows his former wife.

Will the next one to stumble into the church be Pele's favorite sister Hiʻiaka? Or maybe the fire goddess herself?

eleven

I'm making my way out of the chapel after the funeral, just turning my phone back on, when it rings.

"Kai?" It's Donnie. "He's in the restroom," she says. "Just to warn you, he wants to drive to Wao Kele O Puna."

"Why?" I ask.

"I don't know," she says. "Memories, I guess. All the rigging and equipment and buildings are gone. There's nothing to see. It's just an empty hole in the rainforest at the end of a lava road."

"The Puna forest is isolated," I say. "It'll be tough to follow you and not be seen. I'll have to lay way back."

"Good idea, Kai. Rex joked on the way over here: 'That guy in the yellow Porsche seems to follow us everywhere.' I guess he must have seen you coming up from Hilo."

I gulp. Ransom's eyes appear not to be aging as fast as the rest of his body. "The Porsche wasn't my idea. The agency was out of all but exotic cars. It was either this or walk."

"Here he comes," she says nervously. "I've got to hang—"

I hurry to the Boxster. Kawika has already pulled up to the chapel door and the Ransoms are climbing into the black limo.

They pull away. I follow at what I hope is enough distance to evade Ransom's view.

In the parking lot we pass an old beat-up truck that has faded letters on the door: LONDON DRILLING EQUIPMENT. Ransom's ex-partner. Smashed Father Time with his flowing beard is inside trying to start the old beast—and not having much luck. Should he be driving in his condition?

I aim the yellow Porsche back onto Crater Rim Drive, well behind the Lincoln. It passes the park entry station and heads down toward Hilo. I let two vehicles come between us, and then follow.

The rainforest. Ransom's going back.

When reaching the town of Kea'au, the limo turns right onto Kea'au-Pāhoa Road. Wao Kele O Puna, the upland rainforest of Puna, is another ten miles almost due south. But first we pass through the quaint town of Pāhoa that looks like a snapshot from the Old West—plank sidewalks under wood-railed balconies and false-front clapboard buildings. The balconies are festooned with bunting and flags and flowers, giving the little town a cheerful, festive feel. But we quickly leave that cheerfulness behind.

I lay back further because now there are no cars between the limo and me. Soon the Lincoln makes a sharp right off Kea'au-Pāhoa Road and heads into the forest. The road eventually turns from asphalt to crushed lava. The Ransoms' car is alone. I try to get lost in its dust contrail.

I slow down and glance from one side of the road to the other, taking in the amazing diversity of the forest that Ransom had so casually disregarded in his effort to exploit the supposed energy sources in its depths: the scarlet flowers of the mossy-trunked 'ōhi'a tree; the pendulous fronds of the *palapalai* clump fern; the soaring umbrella-like *hapu'u* tree fern; the silver-leafed and orange blossomed *pa'iniu* lily; and the smooth, shiny twining leaves of the fragrant *maile* vine. These trees, ferns, flowers, and vines in the rainforest, protesters argued, were vital to native Hawaiian gathering rights and cultural practices—from securing natural remedies to making *lei* and adornments for sacred *hula*. The SPC sought to reclaim what they believed was rightfully theirs.

Into this culturally rich and fragile ecosystem Ransom brought his drilling operation, apparently ignoring the traditional admonition to tread lightly and treasure this wonder of nature.

> *E nihi ka hele i ka uka o Puna,*
> *mai 'ako i ka pua*
> *o lilo i ke alao ka hewahewa*

> Approach cautiously the forests of Puna,
> do not pluck flowers lest
> you be lost in the pathways of error.

After a mile or two of thick forest, a clearing comes into view. The limo drives straight in. I pull off into a break in the road. I park the Boxster between two *'ōhi'a* trees, hoping Ransom on his way out won't spot the yellow roadster among the bright red *lehua* blooms canopying the trees.

Stepping back onto the road, I gaze into the hole in the forest and recall news coverage of the drilling and the protests. The clear-cut, geometrical scar of nearly eight acres looks hauntingly familiar—like a science fiction movie in which a giant flying saucer has landed and scorched the earth.

The rigid straight lines and totally denuded landscape in the midst of lush greenery bring to mind the opposing camps that spurred the protests. Those who would preserve and protect the land vs. those who would exploit and develop it. There wasn't much middle ground between these champions of untamed nature and champions of untamed industry.

On one corner of these barren acres sits an eerily square reservoir of milky zinc green. I don't know what chemicals the reservoir contains or what purpose it served, but its murky surface looks as unnatural as the stripped land.

I hear something that makes me turn around. Another car raising dust pulls up about twenty yards behind me. The driver climbs out. A Touch of Grey. *He's everywhere.* He just stands by his car, looking past me to the Ransoms. He must wonder about me like I wonder about him.

I turn back to the clearing in the forest and watch the old man step from the limo, hobble with his cane a few paces toward the green pond, then stop in his tracks and scan the entire clearing. I can't see the expression on his face. He's too far away. But I can see him shrug as if to say, "What was all this about?" I imagine him reflecting on his drilling on the disputed land, the anger and resentment it aroused, and then the ultimate failure of his operation to produce enough steam and energy to be profitable.

Why he wanted to return here is anybody's guess. Could it be that his ill health and the death of two of his former executives have heightened his feelings of mortality? Or is he merely lamenting that fate defeated his reign as the geothermal king?

He shakes his head. He bows. He moves closer to that milky pond, almost stumbles, and his wife dashes from the limo to right him. She turns him around, guiding him back to the car. They both climb in. I hide among the 'ōhi'a trees when the limo passes, raising a dust cloud. A Touch of Grey briefly disappears among the trees, then jumps into his car and raises a dust cloud of his own. I fire up the Boxster and follow both dust clouds back to the Volcano House.

* * *

Tuesday evening the Ransoms leave me alone. Donnie calls once to say they are dining in their room. I'm relieved and re-pack my bag. Their flight to Kāua'i via Honolulu departs at noon. Except for following the Ransoms back to Hilo tomorrow morning, I'm done. Well, I'll continue to keep an eye out for A Touch of Grey—*whoever he is.*

I phone Ashley in Denver again. And leave another message. I want to ask her about the Hawaiian bracelet with her name on it I found at the scene of the Pali crash, and about the party she attended celebrating the Lindquist twins' twenty-first birthday. Frustrating as it is not to hear from Ashley, I'm glad to have a case waiting for me when I return to Maunakea Street. And also glad to put this glorified chaperone gig behind me.

I eat alone that night. On my way back from the hotel restaurant I walk by the Ransoms' room. I hear tapping and stop. The tapping seems to be coming from the room next door. Is it the toe tap of a hotel guest listening to music? Or maybe some kind of secret code?

Or just my overactive imagination?

twelve

Wednesday morning, I'm awakened by a call. I was wrong. Donnie does need my services. She says her husband insists on walking the Crater Rim Trail again before breakfast. For his health, she tells me. And he's going alone. She doesn't say why. No worries, I reply. I'll be waiting for him by the trail.

Same drill as before. I hide behind the corner of the hotel when Ransom appears. The old man hobbles out the side door, makes his way awkwardly across the lawn with his cane, and sets out even more slowly than before—with no one now to support his feeble progress. I let him get ahead of me, far enough so he won't think he's being followed, but not so far that I lose sight of him.

The air is chilly and thick with mist. The sky is ghostly white. Visibility is even worse than yesterday. We're walking in a cloud. Double exposures, odd outlines, and shrouded images distort even the most familiar objects. I stick close to Ransom. He shouldn't be left alone in this murk.

I look behind me. No Touch of Grey in the parade. To track Ransom today he'd have to be close. He's not. Why go to so much trouble to follow a man and then just quit?

Not me. I'm still on the case. I follow Ransom, just the two of us, alone on the trail. Not even any other tourists at this hour. We leave the Volcano House behind and head into the tree ferns. The old man is under those green umbrellas when he puts his cell phone to his ear. He talks briefly, and then hangs up.

He hobbles on. Finally he reaches The Steaming Bluff, the goal of his solo hike. He stops at the first gaping vent and leans against the top guardrail. The steam, billowing thick with sulfur, still appears to be the most visible threat to his wellbeing.

A young woman approaches him from the opposite direction. Even through the steam I can tell she's oddly dressed for the trail: flowing crimson gown, shimmering black hair, flame-red lipstick, and eyes vivid with dark shadow and liner. She's attired more for a prom than a hike. Ransom sees her and they appear to lock eyes briefly.

Who is this woman? She looks hauntingly like a well-known *kinolau* of Pele. Donnie mentioned this guise of the goddess in my office—the seductive young woman in red. My client didn't describe her in detail. She didn't need to. Like most people who grow up in the islands, I know. That *kinolau* and this woman on the trail appear to be one and the same.

Can't be. I scratch my head. Is she why the old man insisted on walking alone? Was the call from her? Or has she merely bumped into him by chance?

Now my own phone rings. It's Donnie. *"Kai!"* She sounds hysterical. *"I'm so afraid!"*

"What's wrong?" I say. "Where are you?"

"I'm running toward you on the trail." She's breathless. "Now I can just barely see you through the mist."

I turn around and see the vague outline of a person, motioning rapidly toward herself.

"I'm so afraid!" Her voice is lower now, but still on the verge of hysteria.

"Wait there." I run to her. I don't like leaving Ransom behind, but he's not so far away that I can't return to him quickly. I keep glancing back as I move further from him and the woman.

When I reach Donnie she's clutching a piece a paper in her trembling hands. She grabs my arm and pulls me a few steps off the trail into the tree ferns, out of sight of her husband.

"What's wrong?"

"This." She hands the paper to me. The words on it are cut and pasted from a newspaper.

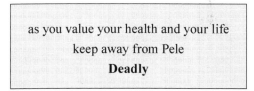

as you value your health and your life
keep away from Pele
Deadly

"Where did you get this?"

"It was slipped under my door just after Rex left," Donnie says, still trembling. "What does it mean?"

"You tell me. You know your husband and his enemies better than I do." I step back onto the trail to catch another glimpse of Ransom. The air is thick and I can barely see the shadowy outlines of two people.

"Maybe it's Rex's ex-wife?" She shrugs.

"What motive would his ex have to produce a note like this? Just to make him, or you, uncomfortable?"

"I don't know." Donnie shakes her head. "I'm so scared, I can't think straight."

I believe her.

Donnie tries again. "Maybe the insane woman who escaped from the mental hospital?"

"No matter who delivered the note," I say, "we can't do anything about it now. I better get back to your husband." I fold and put the note in the pocket of my aloha shirt and start with a quick stride toward Ransom. Donnie's next words stop me.

"I warned Rex already," she says.

"That was you who called him?" *There goes my theory about the woman.*

"He told me I was worrying about nothing. Then he hung up."

From the direction of The Steaming Bluff I hear what sounds like a thud and a groan. Donnie seems too out of it to notice.

"Why don't you go back to your room now and let me handle this?" I say. But I'm not waiting for an answer. I'm already moving through the mist.

I start running. I race through the fern grove. I can hardly see my own feet. But I keep going.

I hear my shoes pounding the trail. Soon I reach The Steaming Bluff. But I don't see him or the woman in red. The vapor is so thick now I can't even make out the caldera below. I approach the vent where I left Ransom. The closer I get, the hotter and more rotten-smelling the steam rising from the cavernous hole. Pele's at it again.

"Mr. Ransom?" I call his name, abandoning my cover.

I doubt the old man could have made it much beyond the vent in the short time I've been gone. But he's nowhere in sight.

I lean against the guardrail, like he did, and peer in. The smell of sulfur suddenly combines with a more noxious odor. The stench of burning flesh.

My eyes follow my nose down into the abyss, blinking to avoid the reeking steam. About a dozen feet down, lodged on an outcropping, lies a man. His skin is lobster pink. His lips are puffy. His eyeballs bulge like poached eggs.

He isn't climbing out on his own. He's been boiled alive.

thirteen

It's him. The man I was hired to protect.

No doubt about it. His cane, already discolored by the searing steam, is wedged in a crack just a few feet below his body.

The woman in red—a dead ringer for Pele—has vanished.

Unreal. My brain rebels. But I have to admit what I saw. And it seems I saw Pele, in the flesh.

Maybe she had nothing to do with it? I rationalize. *Maybe Ransom just got too close, succumbed to the fumes, and stumbled into the vent?*

I shake my head. I walk in slow circles, trying to figure out what to do. Then I get a grip on myself.

Survey the scene.

I'm the first one here and presumably nothing has been touched. It's not often a PI gets first crack like this. It may sound cold, since the old man is lying in the vent, but there's nothing I can do about that. What I can do is try to find out why he died. And what, if anything, the woman in red had to do with it.

I scan the trail near the vent. The hard-packed dirt, trodden by countless park visitors, reveals no discrete shoe- or footprints. Neither Ransom's nor the young woman's. Just off the trail I notice a broken 'ōhelo branch and small depressions in the vegetation that suggest someone scrambled through the brush toward Crater Rim Drive, about fifty yards away. The woman? Unlikely, given her attire.

My first look gets me nowhere.

When I'm satisfied I've combed the scene the best I can in short order, I dial 911. I'll wait to inform Donnie until the Park Service arrives.

Within minutes a smoky-the-bear hat shows up. It's Ranger Crisp. He peers into the vent. He asks me the expected questions. He's calm and deliberate. I give him my card and explain that I've been following Mr. Ransom incognito and why. Then the ranger calls in emergency services.

Seconds later, A Touch of Grey shows up. He sees the former CEO at the bottom of the vent, looks at the ranger and me, and asks, "What happened?"

"We're not sure yet," Ranger Crisp says. "Do you know this man?"

"I know who he is," he replies. "I'm with Puna Security." He also hands the ranger a card. "I've been shadowing Mr. Ransom."

"On whose orders?" the ranger asks.

"A former exec of Mr. Ransom's company—an old friend of his—hired me to follow him because of what happened to Mr. Nagahara and Mr. Kroften."

"With the victim's blessing?"

"He didn't know."

"So that makes two of you tailing him?" The ranger says. "And neither of you saw what happened?"

"I almost did. The old man was approached by a woman." I describe her and her resemblance to Pele. "Then Mrs. Ransom, my client, called me away for a moment." I save the warning note until I can discuss it privately with the ranger. "When I returned, the woman was gone and he was in the vent."

The Puna Security man chimes in just as my cell phone rings. It's Donnie.

"Kai," she says, "Where's Rex? He should be back from his walk by now."

"Stay where you are," I say. "I'll be right there."

I hang up and tell the two men I'm going to inform the deceased's wife. That's normally the job of the official investigating agency, but since the ranger isn't about to leave the body, he does not object. I hike back to the Volcano House. On the way to her room I stop at the front desk and ask Pualani to photocopy the note.

Pualani glances at it and is comfortable enough with our friendship to read it silently. I watch her lips move as she reaches last word and whispers *Pele.* She gives me a look as mysterious as her earlier wink, places the note on her machine, and then hands back the original and copy.

I say, *"Mahalo,"* and put both in my shirt pocket.

I knock on Donnie's door and she lets me in. From the look of concern on her face I can tell she already knows something is wrong. No sense beating around the bush.

"I'm sorry to inform you," I say, "that your husband is dead."

She buries her face in her hands and starts to sob. "I knew we shouldn't come here! I knew Pele would get him!"

I put my hand on her shoulder. "I'm very sorry."

She keeps her face buried in her hands. She seems resigned rather than shocked. She doesn't ask how it happened or where. She just sobs.

"Your husband wasn't well," I say. "He might have had another heart attack, even if he didn't come to the Volcano

House." I don't mention the woman in red. Donnie doesn't need to hear about her now.

"I want to go to him," she says. "I want to be with Rex."

"It's not a pretty sight. I'll take you if you want, but it's not a pretty sight."

"I don't care." She goes into the bathroom and rinses her face.

Then we walk the Crater Rim Trail to where Ranger Crisp and the Puna Security man have now been joined by a dozen onlookers, a state sheriff, and an emergency staff in rescue garb resembling space suits. They've got ropes and pulleys and other equipment. Ransom is still down in the vent. He's not going anywhere.

"Are you sure you want to see this, Donnie?"

"I don't want to," she says. "I have to. Rex is my husband."

"Okay." I take her to the edge of the trail. She peers over the railing and into the vent. "I knew it would happen!" she cries. "I knew it!"

"We better go," I say.

"I need to talk to her," the ranger says to me. "The sooner the better."

"She'll be in her room. This is no place for her now."

The ranger nods and looks at me. "I need to talk more to you too."

"Whenever you're ready," I say and lead the widow of Rex Ransom back to the Volcano House.

fourteen

"You should show this to the ranger when he interviews you." I hand Donnie the original note when we return to her room, keeping the copy in my pocket. She scans it once again.

"Once the ranger is through with us, would you like me to accompany you back to Kāua'i?" I ask. "Sorry to say, your husband's body may have to stay here with the medical examiner for now."

"That's very kind of you," she says. "I'll manage, but can you wait while I make a call?"

"No problem," I say, assuming she's going to inform family members of her husband's death.

When she takes her cell phone from her purse, I excuse myself. "I'll be out in the hall."

"Stay here," she says. "I'm just calling our renter, Jeffrey Bywater. I don't want him to be shocked when he watches tonight's news on the cruise ship." She punches in a number she seems to know by heart.

"Hello, Jeffrey? This is Donnie."

She pauses. I hear a male voice on the other end of the line, but I can't make out his words. She whispers to me, "He's aboard the *Pride of Aloha*."

"Are you and Byron enjoying the cruise?"

He responds in more words I can't decipher.

"I'm glad," she says. "Jeffrey, I'm afraid I have some bad news. Rex apparently had another heart attack while he was walking a trail by the Volcano House. He was found in a steam vent." She pauses. "Jeffrey, he's dead."

I overhear Jeffrey telling someone what Donnie just said. The other person, I assume, is Byron, Jeffrey's friend.

Donnie starts to sob again. "I'll be okay," she says into the phone. "I just wanted you to know." Another pause. "That's not necessary. I'll be fine. I'm with the private detective."

She puts her hand on mine. I wonder what's going on.

"Okay, do what you like, but it's not necessary. Goodbye, Jeffrey."

She puts down her phone.

"Jeffrey and Byron have decided to cut their cruise short," she explains. "They're going to leave the ship when it docks at Nāwiliwili Harbor on Kāua'i tomorrow morning, pick me up at Lihue Airport, and drive me back to Hanalei. I told them it wasn't necessary. But they're such caring guys."

"Sounds like you'll be in good hands," I say, but am frankly relieved she no longer needs my services.

"I'll be fine to fly back to Kāua'i by myself tomorrow morning," she explains, "since both of them will meet me there."

She barely gets out her words when there's a knock at her door. I open it to Ranger Crisp. He wants to interview Donnie first. Alone. So I step into the hall. The ranger tells me, "Don't go far."

"I'll be in the lobby," I say.

Soon I'm warming my bones by the perpetual flames of the famous fireplace. Time passes. I'm not thinking about Rex Ransom. Maybe his death is too gruesome. The crackle and piney scent of the fire makes my mind wander—back to the Pali case and those unreturned calls, back to Blossom and her abusive ex-boyfriend, back to Maile and Kula. I drift off into a reverie that's suddenly interrupted.

"I'm ready for you," the ranger says.

We walk into the hotel dining room, empty at this time of day, take a table, and the interview begins.

Ranger Crisp proceeds to ask me more expected questions, this time to corroborate what he's been told by Donnie. How long I'd been working for her. What my duties entailed. Who I was protecting Mr. Ransom from. And how I went about it. The ranger also asks about the last time I saw Ransom. He seems to assume I'm the last person to see the victim alive. But I know I'm not.

I mention again the young woman in red. "It may sound crazy, but this woman looked amazingly like Pele in one of her guises. It's probably just a coincidence."

"Stanger things have happened," the ranger says. "Some people will say Pele has claimed another victim, because of Mr. Ransom's role in the geothermal operation at Wao Kele O Puna. His death makes three. And three looks like a pattern."

"And then there's the note," I say. "I assume Mrs. Ransom showed it to you."

"She did," the ranger says. "We'll follow up on it."

"Pele wasn't Mr. Ransom's only enemy—real or imagined," I say. "He had mortal enemies too, but you probably know that."

"We know about some others. Who did you have in mind?"

I tell him.

He nods in agreement, as if we have the same list. Then he says, "Park Service personnel just removed the body."

"I bet his wallet was found on him," I say, "with no evidence of theft."

The ranger nods. "We're going on the assumption, suggested by Mrs. Ransom, that her husband had a heart attack. The autopsy will determine the exact cause."

"I would have been there," I say, "but she was hysterical about that note."

"It's a sad coincidence, isn't it?"

"How's that?"

"Well, she hires you to protect him. You follow him everywhere and nothing happens. And then you leave him alone for barely a minute—to comfort her—and he turns up dead."

Before long the interview is over. I walk back to Donnie's room to express my sympathy again and say goodbye. She's not there. Just as well.

Minutes later my overnight bag rides beside me in the yellow Boxster, heading down the Volcano Highway to Hilo Airport.

fifteen

Thursday I get in early to my office with a copy of the morning paper. The front page poses a provocative question: "Pele's Third Victim?" Below is a photo of a younger Rex Ransom in his geothermal days. And below that, instructions to turn to the local section for the full story. I do.

> **Pele's Third Victim?**
> **Another Former Ransom Geothermal Executive Dies**
> Hilo: Big Island geothermal developer Rex Ransom was found dead yesterday morning in an active steam vent at Hawai'i Volcanoes National Park. The former CEO of Ransom Geothermal Enterprises apparently fell into the vent after being overcome by fumes. He was walking by himself on the Crater Rim Trail near the Volcano House when he fell.

Ransom and his wife were staying in the park while attending a funeral for attorney Stanley Nagahara, who once represented Ransom Geothermal. Nagahara's body was discovered recently in a crevasse in the East Rift Zone after a solo hiking accident. Nagahara was the second former Ransom Geothermal executive to die in the park. Drilling engineer Karl Kroften died nearly two years ago in a single car accident near the Halemaʻumaʻu Crater.

Ransom's death yesterday brings the number to three. The men's connection with the controversial geothermal project in the Wao Kele O Puna rainforest has not been lost on devotees of Pele, legendary goddess of fire and volcanoes.

"Pele get her revenge," said one lifelong Puna resident who asked not to be identified.

But a Park Service spokesman explained that steam vent deaths are not unexampled. "This has happened before," said Ranger Benjamin Cabato, referring to a park volunteer who died from a fall into a steam vent in 1992.

The young woman in red. She's not mentioned. Just as Pele devotees saw the goddess in the grey-haired old woman with her white dog climbing into Karl Kroften's BMW before it crashed, so too would they see the goddess in the young woman who appeared before Rex Ransom fell.

But I have no time to dwell on the newspaper. I have to put Ransom's death out of my mind. The Pali case needs attention.

I take the orange shag stairs down into the flower shop. Blossom is not there. But Mrs. Fujiyama is, tidying a refrigerated display case filled with fragrant *pīkake*, plumeria, and white ginger *lei.*

"Morning, Mrs. Fujiyama." I whiff the perfumed air. *Lucky you live Hawai'i.* Where else can a PI hang his shingle above a *lei* shop?

"Good morning, Mr. Cooke." She glances at me over her half glasses, always politely formal, and smiles. If she's still worried about Junior, she's not showing it.

I hustle to my parking garage. Maunakea Street is in peak form as I step onto the early morning sidewalk. The floral scents of the *lei* shop are soon replaced by other aromas of Chinatown: the reek of the open dumpster against Mrs. Fujiyama's building, the tropical tang of mangos on a fruit vendor's cart, the earthy scent of *bok choy* and other Chinese cabbages at a vegetable stall, the sweet-sour smell of *char siu* hanging in a lunch counter window, the pungent waft of the morning's catch in the fish market; and the cheap perfume of a lady of the evening strolling home from her night's work on Hotel Street.

Before long I'm leaving Chinatown behind, driving down Maunakea to Nimitz Highway. I turn right and glance back at the Aloha Tower—no *Pride of Aloha* today. Donnie Ransom's tenant, Jeffrey, and his friend Byron no doubt by now have disembarked at Nāwiliwili Harbor and retrieved their landlady at Lihue Airport. I'm off the hook because of those two guys. And glad the whole Ransom mess is behind me.

I turn off Nimitz Highway on Māpunapuna Street, drive a few blocks *mauka*, and pull in front of HPD's contract vehicle impound lot, operated by Stonehenge Recoveries. On any given day on the island of Oʻahu more vehicles are towed than can be accommodated on police property. So one lucky towing company wins the lucrative contract to perform this function. I got a green light from my friend in blue, Creighton Lee, to visit Stonehenge Recoveries.

Stonehenge. Curious name for a Honolulu wrecking yard. Does the name allude to that prehistoric circle of mammoth stones outside London town, in the direction of Dartmoor? *Never been, but would like to go.* Maybe the tow company wants patrons to think solid and reputable and enduring?

The yard itself is not much to write home about. A double-wide trailer, with a couple of wrecked cars in front of it, serves as an office. The office has two windows where you can pay your fine and liberate your car. By the windows are instructions in big red letters telling you what forms to fill out and how to pay.

Speaking of luck, as I step from my car some unlucky guy is standing at one of the windows, arguing with the unlovely woman on the other side. She *looks* okay. What's unlovely about her is her tongue. The poor guy whose automobile she holds hostage is getting an earful. She's grown thick skin, I guess. Dealing with irate motorists day after day can do that. She's telling him he owes not only a fine, but also a towing and a storage charge. She's telling him he must pay it all in full and in cash before he sees his car again.

He objects. She has an answer for everything: You think the charges are unfair? Fill out a complaint form. You want a copy of your completed form? Sorry, no copies. You've heard complaint forms mysteriously disappear? Can't be. We carefully file every form and act on it promptly. Any other questions?

Now he's fuming. Soon the unlucky guy at the window and the woman on the other side are really going at it. She doesn't even see me as I slip by the doublewide trailer and walk behind it into the impound lot. Despite my friend in blue's assistance, technically I'm not supposed to be here. But I don't let that stop me. I'm poor at following rules and regulations.

It's a clear March morning and the metallic paint on dozens of impounded cars sparkles in the sun. The car I'm looking for won't have much sparkle left. It won't have much of anything left. Vehicles involved in serious accidents are typically winched onto a flatbed truck, sometimes in pieces. That's what happened in the Pali crash, after the Honda Civic plunged from the cliff. I've seen photos of the wreck, but not the actual vehicle. Until now.

I'm not a curious onlooker or morbid spectator hovering over a wreck that killed three people. My mission is different. I'm looking for material evidence for a civil trial, much the same sort of evidence I looked for at the scene of the crash: cash register and credit card receipts, bottles (intact or broken), clothing or pieces of clothing, shoes, slippers, fluid and other stains—anything that might pertain to the accident. Like that Hawaiian bracelet belonging to Ashley. She still hasn't returned my calls. So I still have no explanation why her bracelet rode in the doomed car when she didn't.

The deeper into the yard I walk, the more desperate the shape of the cars. There must be a hundred here, easy. At the very back are the worst cases—whose makes and models are almost impossible to determine. This is where I find the remains of the metallic red Honda, looking less like a car than a coffin.

Why am I always on the trail of death?

Fireball really did a job. The only way to tell that this mangled mess is a Honda is a bent badge on what remains of the hood. The car's sides are sheared almost flat from slamming the walls of the Pali tunnels. Its roof is crushed nearly to the windowsills. Its windshield pillars flattened to the dashboard. All the glass is gone.

Inside is a world of hurt. Two deflated airbags sag to the floor, dotted with dried blood. Bloodstains on the passenger seats must belong to the birthday twins; stains on the driver seat to Fireball.

I reach into the car, wishing I was wearing latex. Gingerly I run my fingers across the discolored seats, looking for anything. Then I stretch into the foot-wells, trying to follow my fingers with my eyes. I come up empty. No receipts. No bottles. No clothing or swatches of cloth.

I turn to the glove box—covered now by one of the deployed airbags. I fold the stained bag up onto the dash and try the glove box's door. It won't budge. No surprise. The Honda has been twisted and torqued by its catastrophic collision. Bare hands won't do. I scan the surrounding wrecks for something to pry open the box. Under an old Pontiac, a classic almost as old as my Impala, I see a piece of broken trim—metal, not plastic—about a foot long. I grab it, wedge it in the uneven seam surrounding the glove box, and pry the door open.

I find what you might expect—an owner's manual, service records, a pen, a little bong pipe. I pull everything out.

Nothing is left in the empty box. Except for one thing. A slip of paper. A cash register receipt

Bingo! But there's not enough readable print on the receipt to tell much. However, there is a phone number on the back. It's written in a woman's hand. No name. Just the number. And it's not a Hawai'i number. Area code 303.

I have no idea where 303 is. But I'm going to find out.

sixteen

Back in my office I get a call from Tommy Woo. I'm sure the first topic of conversation is going to be the death of Rex Ransom at Volcano House.

I'm wrong. Tommy starts off: "Hey Kai, did you hear the one about the sushi bar on Bishop Street that caters exclusively to lawyers?"

"No, Tommy." *Another lawyer joke?*

"It's called Sosumi," he says. "You get it? *So sue me.*"

After Tommy reels off a few more I finally bring up the Ransoms. "I wonder how Donnie will make out."

"Just fine," Tommy says. "Ransom had lots of money and Donnie has lots of time to spend it."

"They seemed devoted," I say. "Well, she and the old man did have their moments."

"You're a choir boy, Kai. How do you make it as a private dick? Ten bucks says she's got a young stud on the side. Watch *The Garden Island* for a wedding announcement."

"What do I know about women?" I admit. "Or weddings?"

"Speaking of weddings," Tommy says, "I'm going to ask Zahra to marry me. What do you think?"

Zahra is Tommy's new girlfriend—a ravishing exchange student from Kenya about half his age whose visa is about to expire. That's probably the reason for the sudden wedding plans.

"I dunno, Tommy," I say. He's been married twice and both marriages were disasters. "You've known her, what, about a month?"

"I knew all I needed to know from day one." Tommy sounds defensive. "Women from Africa have souls a mile deep."

I just listen. I don't want to dig myself deeper. Plus I'm sure Tommy is savvy enough not to get taken in by an immigration scam.

"Sorry I brought it up." Now Tommy sounds hurt.

I try to recover. "You have my blessing—I wish you two every happiness."

"*Shibai,*" he says and hangs up.

And I'm thinking: *What crazy things people do for love.*

After Tommy's call I try the number I found in the glove box of Fireball's crushed Honda. But first I look up the area code—303. It's Denver.

Ashley. She flew to Denver on the night of the accident.

It's not her cell number—I check—which has a Hawai'i area code—808.

When I dial the 303 number I'm thinking I may get lucky and Ashley will be on the other end. I really need to talk to her.

The number rings and rings. Finally voicemail kicks in. "Hi, this is Ethan," says a twenty-something male voice. "Please leave me a message."

"Hi Ethan," I say. *Who the heck is Ethan?* "My name is Kai Cooke. I'm a private detective in Honolulu. I'm trying to locate a girl named Ashley who may be able to help me with a case I'm working on—an auto accident on Oʻahu that killed Heather and Lindsay Lindquist. Do you know Ashley or the twins? Yes or no, either way, would you please give me a call?"

I leave my phone number and hang up—hoping I'm getting closer to the elusive Ashley.

On my way out of the office later that day I stop in the *lei* shop and ask Blossom how things are going. She's a good kid and I fear for her.

"Junior scares me." She trains her luminous eyes on me. "Sometimes he hurts me."

I gaze upon her reed-like figure and long brown hair thinking, *No woman—young or old—deserves that punk.*

Mrs. Fujiyama overhears our conversation and steps to the *lei* table.

"Junior—bad man," she says. "He keep coming back. What I can do?"

I try to reassure her. "A TRO may help."

"TRO—what that?" she asks.

"Temporary Restraining Order," I explain. "It's a legal document that will forbid Junior to come near Blossom or your shop."

"Piece of papah," she says. "What good dat? How one papah stop angry man?"

I see her point. "I'll keep an eye out for him," I say.

No sooner do I say that than a dusty black pickup truck with big knobby tires screeches to a stop in front of the shop. Junior storms in. A floral funeral wreath on a tripod awaiting a bereaved family comes crashing down. Mrs. Fujiyama watches in horror as perfectly arranged flowers break loose and roll across the floor. A silken banner—OUR BELOVED MOTHER—twirls in the air on its way down.

Blossom's ex has a scowl on his face and he's coming fast. Blossom grips me. *Does he think I'm her new guy?*

Blossom screams. Mrs. Fujiyama runs for the shop phone. Then I realize Junior's not coming for Blossom. He's coming for me.

He takes a jab at me with his right fist. Since my arms are shielding Blossom, all I can do is turn away. He catches me on the side of my face, just above my left eye. It's a glancing blow but breaks the skin. The results are instantaneous. My blood drips onto Blossom's hair.

I release Blossom, rise from the table, and start for him. Mrs. Fujiyama comes back with the phone in her hand. "Police," she says in a surprisingly calm voice.

When Junior sees Mrs. Fujiyama talking on the phone, he runs for the door. Then he turns back and glares at me. "Nex' time I *kill* you."

He jumps into his black truck and tears away, smoking the tires down Maunakea Street.

Blossom collapses on the *lei* table. Mrs. Fujiyama comforts her. I'm not seeing so well, as blood fills my left eye. I grab for my handkerchief and daub the wound. The broken skin only stings. But the volume of red is amazing. It must look worse than it feels because Mrs. Fujiyama calls my name repeatedly: "Mr. Cooke! Mr. Cooke!"

"I'm okay," I tell her.

I barely get these words out when I hear sirens and then two HPD officers charge into the shop. They look at me and one says to the other, "Call EMS." I try to talk them out of this, but the other officer takes my arm and sits me down in one of the *lei* girl's chairs.

"Take it easy, sir," he says. "Help is on the way."

I don't bother to dissuade him. I just sit and wait. Somehow one of the officers produces a small towel and I bury my bloody face in it.

"What happened here?" the first officer asks Mrs. Fujiyama and her girls.

They start to explain. I try to talk, but the officer who handed me the towel puts his hand on my shoulder and says, "You can give a statement later."

So I just listen. Mrs. Fujiyama explains and fills out a witness statement. Junior is in trouble. He's looking at assault and battery, terroristic threatening, and property damage. In addition to outstanding warrants, he's also violated the terms of his parole, which stems from arrest and incarceration for domestic abuse of his girlfriend before Blossom. When HPD catches him, he's going back to jail. No question. But while he's still on the outside he's going to be all the more desperate and dangerous.

Another siren. Soon through my clouded vision I see flashing lights in front Mrs. Fujiyama's shop. Two medical techs rush in, see my bloody hand towel, and kneel down in front of me.

"We better get that looked at by a doc," one says.

"I'll be fine," I say. "It's just a scratch."

"We can't take you against your will, sir," says the other, "but you really should have it looked at."

I nod.

They put me on a gurney, wheel me to the ambulance, with Mrs. Fujiyama and her *lei* girls looking on. I should feel like a hero.

Before long we're at Queens Medical Center emergency room. The good thing about coming to the hospital in an ambulance is that you get to see someone immediately. I'm quickly processed and put on an examination table behind drawn curtains. A nurse has me remove my bloody shirt and then a doc looks me over. The nurse cleans the wound. Whatever she uses makes it sting again. Then the doc shines a floodlight on it and looks closely.

"Well, you're in luck," he says. "An adhesive strip should do the trick. No stitches today. Unless you want some?" He cracks a smile.

What's with the humor of ER doctors? I almost say

"Stay out of the ocean for a few days," he says. "You're a surfer, right?"

"Yeah, how'd you know?"

"Those teeth marks on your chest," he says. "Dead giveaway."

My shark bite. I don't like his choice of words. But I repeat: "Stay out of the ocean."

After a cab ride I'm back at the office with more adhesive strips and ointment and a list of instructions. When I check myself out in the mirror in the closet-sized bathroom used by Mrs. Fujiyama's five office tenants, I'm surprised that the strip the nurse put on my forehead camouflages the entire wound.

I get off easy. But I keep hearing Junior's menacing voice inside my head: "Nex' time I *kill* you!"

seventeen

By Friday Ashley still hasn't returned my call. Neither has the guy named Ethan. *Does nobody in Denver return calls?* I'm wondering even harder now why Ashley's Hawaiian bracelet was at the scene of the accident when she wasn't riding in the doomed car, and why Ethan's phone number was in the glove box. I could leave each another message, but in my experience too many messages can make witnesses less willing to talk. In-person interviews are always best, but difficult when the persons are in Denver and I'm in Honolulu.

So I face a stack of papers on my desk begging to be filed, and prepare a bill for Donnie Ransom. I have feelings about billing her so soon after her husband's death—a death I was hired to prevent—but I get over them. The charge on my credit card for the three-day rental for the Boxster alone is over a grand.

Before Friday is over, the bill is in the mail to Kāua'i and I'm glad to put the Volcano House case behind me.

On Saturday, against my own advice, I leave two more voicemails for Denver. I don't expect to hear soon from Ashley and Ethan, given recent history. But I've got to make something happen. Even if I have to resort to something unorthodox—like hiring an undercover operative.

A young guy I know named Nicholas, an apprentice carpenter, really likes his beer. Nicholas is a big guy and looks older than his years. He's just shy of twenty-one, the legal drinking age in Hawai'i. Since it's Saturday, he'll be knocking back a few. I give him a call and make him an offer he can't refuse. Today Nicholas is working for me.

I pick up Nicholas at the house off Kapahulu Avenue in Kaimuki he shares with another guy and a girl. I beep and he ambles out with an open beer in his hand. He's got a big smile on his face, like he's the happiest twenty-year-old on earth. Twenty year olds have a lot to be happy about.

"Hey, Nick," I say, as he steps into the car. "Leave the beer here."

"Shoots, Kai." He sets the open bottle in the street. "Geev' me five, *braaahh!*" The way he's talking makes me wonder if he's up to the task. But there's no use doubting or turning back now. He's my best shot.

I give him a high-five and ask: "You ready?"

"*Right on!*" he says. And then: "Thanks again, man, for findin' my tools. I hope that guy that took 'em gets twenty freakin' years."

Nicholas is referring to the favor I did him. Somebody took a bunch of tools from his pickup truck. I tracked down the thief, tipped off HPD on where to find him, and recovered most of the tools. I doubt he'll get much more than probation, but at least I nabbed him.

Once Nicholas is buckled in, I aim my old Impala toward downtown Honolulu to a club called the Lollipop Lounge. En route I give Nick instructions.

"Now here's what you do," I say. "You walk into the Lollipop, take a seat, and order a beer. Give the server your credit card when she brings the beer, and make sure you don't leave without your signed receipt. Get the server's name, if you can. I'll come in after you, take another table, order a beer myself, and watch what happens. If you get carded, the game is up. We'll try another club."

"Got it," he says. "My kind of work!"

When we get to the Lollipop Lounge, on a seedy block of Kona Street not far from Ala Moana Shopping Center, Nicholas follows my instructions to a tee. We're in luck. Business is slow, late on a Saturday afternoon, and he doesn't get carded. Nor does the server, a woman twice Nick's age, notice that he's already had enough to drink.

We're here for a reason. I'm tying to establish that this club serves minors and intoxicated patrons. The Lollipop is the last club that served Heather and Lindsay Lindquist the night they died. The Lollipop also served the driver of the car.

Luck stays with us. I observe Nick, who is underage, being served when he is already clearly buzzed. I observe him using his credit card and getting a receipt. The receipt will have the time and date stamped on it and, of course, Nick's own signature. For good measure, I also buy a beer and pay with my credit card, getting the name of the server from a tag that says STORMY, in the event Nick doesn't.

If the case goes to trial, and the Lollipop is a defendant, I may be deposed to present this evidence against their claims of not serving either the Lindquist twins or Fireball when they were intoxicated. If we're really lucky the same server who served Nicholas was working the night the twins died.

I let Nicholas stay for a second beer, while I nurse the one I ordered. At the bottom of his second, I gesture to him to meet me outside. He does and I drive him home. The beer he left in the street in front of his Kaimuki house is still standing there.

"Take this inside," I say to Nick. "T'anks, brah."

He picks up the bottle, nods, and wobbles into his house. I'd feel bad about contributing to the delinquency of a minor if it wasn't in the interest of stopping the kind of illegal practices that get other minors killed.

On the way back to my apartment on Ala Wai Boulevard my cell phone rings. It's against the law in the City and County of Honolulu to talk on a hand-held cell phone while operating a motor vehicle. But when I think a call may be crucial sometimes I bend that law. If this one is from Denver I really need to take it. I look in my rearview mirror. An HPD cruiser, a white Crown Victoria, is right behind me. *Damn!* I don't even look at caller ID. I let the phone ring.

I can only hope if this call is from Ashley or Ethan that she or he leaves a message. One or both may have information that could help me wrap up the Pali case. But there's nothing I can do now. That HPD cruiser is still riding my bumper.

About a minute later my cell phone beeps. *Phew.* I have a new voicemail. Once I pull into my parking spot at the Edgewater I dial my voicemail and hear a young woman's voice. *Ashley at last?*

"Hello, Kai," she says. A promising start. "May I see you on Monday?"

Better than I expected. But the message doesn't sound right. Why would Ashley ask to see me in my office? All I requested was a return phone call. Plus, the pleasant female voice sounds sophisticated, with none of the rising pitch at sentence endings—*Like everything is a question, you know?*—of Heather and Lindsay Lindquist's other friends I've interviewed.

Then comes the answer.

"My name is Caitlin Ransom. I'm Rex Ransom's daughter."

Rex Ransom's daughter wants to see me?

"I understand you were with my father at Hawai'i Volcanoes National Park. I would like to talk with you about . . ." she pauses, "his death." Then an even longer pause. "Sorry, this is hard for me."

I try to remember if I have a box of tissues in my office. This could be a tearful meeting.

Caitlin Ransom leaves her number in that lovely voice and says she hopes to hear from me soon. I call her back immediately. The phone rings and then her voicemail kicks in.

"Aloha, Caitlin," I say. "Kai Cooke. I'd be happy to see you on Monday. Around nine? If that's okay, no need to call back. I'm very sorry about your father."

I hang up. *And wonder.*

eighteen

On Sunday morning we still have vog and I still haven't heard from Denver. But I'm still stoked about scoring big with Nicholas at the Lollipop Lounge.

I'm hanging out this morning at the Waikīkī Edgewater with the Sunday newspaper. When I was a *keiki,* Sunday was family day. My mom and dad and I would take a picnic to the beach, go for a hike or a drive, or visit my auntie's *ohana* in Punaluʻu. It didn't really matter what we did—as long as we did it together.

I scan the front page. I don't have a problem with being alone on Sunday. I can always go surfing. Never mind the scratch over my eye. Never mind doctor's orders.

I flip pages to the local news and see this:

> **Geothermal CEO Overcome by Fumes**
>
> Hilo: A Big Island medical examiner retained by the National Park Service has determined that former geothermal pioneer Rex Ransom, who died last Wednesday at Hawaiʻi Volcanoes National Park, was overcome by toxic fumes before he

apparently slipped into an active steam vent. Ransom, 70, was discovered in the vent last Wednesday. Volcanic fumes, said the examiner, Elton K. Tamura, MD, can be especially hazardous to the elderly, and to those with heart and lung conditions.

The former CEO of Ransom Geothermal Enterprises, a previous heart attack victim, was by himself on the Crater Rim Trail near the Volcano House when the accident occurred. The day before, he and his wife attended the funeral of former Ransom Geothermal attorney Stanley Nagahara, who also died recently in the park. Another member of the firm, Karl Kroften, died two years ago near the Halemaʻumaʻu Crater.

The deaths of three people closely associated with the controversial geothermal project two decades ago in the Wao Kele O Puna rainforest continues to cause speculation among devotees of Pele that the legendary goddess of volcanoes had a hand in the deaths. The medical examiner's report on the cause of Ransom's death has not put this speculation to rest.

Overcome by fumes? You'd think that would quiet talk of Pele's revenge. Or would it? Was I right to think Ransom's worst threat was the noxious air near the craters?

Still no mention of the young woman in red who approached Ransom on the trail before he died. Or the warning note. Should I bring these up at my Monday meeting with Ransom's daughter?

The Volcano House case just won't go away. Sitting around on Sunday morning doesn't help. I slip on my board shorts and grab my wax. Hard to believe I haven't been in the water since going to the Big Island. *Sorry, Doc.*

Then I get a better idea. Why not take the golden boy? *If Maile will return my call.* I grab my cell, punch in her number, and take a breath. She won't answer. But I'm used to that.

Her phone rings and then I hear her warm familiar voice: "Hi, you've reached Maile Barnes, tracer of missing pets. How can I help?" *If she only knew.*

"Hi, Maile. It's me again. Okay if I take Kula surfing? Been a while since the boy's been in the water. Would you please give me a call? It's now"—I check my watch—"almost nine on Sunday morning. I can pick him up in thirty minutes."

I could say a few other things about missing her and hoping she forgives me, but I don't. She's heard it all. I just say goodbye.

Now the waiting game. I'm stuck until I hear from Maile.

So I reflect on how I messed up. I finally reconnect with the woman of my dreams. And then the relationship goes up in smoke. I could blame it all on Madison Highcamp. She told Maile in a drunken phone call that she—Madison and I—were engaged. It was a lie, but the message stung. Maile had been burned before. She said *never again.* I tried explaining, but no dice. My mistake was not breaking up with Madison sooner. No, my mistake was dating the rich, idle, tycoon's wife in the first place.

My phone beeps. It's a text message from Maile: "OK. Kula in yard."

That's it.

The ex-K9 cop is conveniently not around when I arrive at her Mānoa cottage. *No surprise.* Maile's feelings run deep. She doesn't get over things quickly. And I have to admit—I hurt her. Kula is like a child of divorce, and I have visitation rights.

I walk around to the back yard and there he is—mane and feathering luminous in the sun. He glides toward me with the grace of a stallion. His blond lashes set off dark brown eyes. *Golden boy.* I open the gate and he sidles up to me.

"Hey, Kula." I stroke his sunny fur. "Let's hit the waves."

He barks. His tail sweeps like a golden plume. *He's stoked already.*

From Maile's carport I fetch the tandem board on perpetual loan from my cousin Alika and strap it on my roof racks. Then Kula and I head for the surf. The retriever sticks his head out the window—fleecy ears flapping in the breeze. He's got a big goofy smile on his face.

Dogs aren't allowed in Waikīkī. That's why we pull into Kaka'ako Waterfront Park, to the uncrowded break called Flies. When Kula hears the waves crashing beyond the dune and smells the salt spray he goes ballistic. A boy after my own heart.

I grab the board and Kula prances over the dune to Flies, at the *Ewa* end of the park. I set the big board in the water and Kula steps onto the nose. He knows his spot. I hop on behind him and paddle toward the break.

The one and only surfer in the lineup this early on Sunday is gazing out to sea. In the distance he sees a set coming. He paddles for it. When the first shoulder-high roller reaches him, he's on it.

I paddle into the spot he leaves behind. Another wave rolls in. I swing the tandem board around and point the nose toward shore. The retriever hunches on the nose. I paddle until I feel the rush of water under the board. The nose drops and the board takes on the steep pitch of the wave. I pop up, turn right, and try to stay in front of the curling lip. Kula balances as I trim the board, keeping his paws spread. He barks and barks. *What a rush!*

When the wave fizzles and the board glides to a stop, I swing the nose around to paddle back into the lineup. Kula suddenly pitches into the water. *Oops.* He swims back like nothing happened, and I help him on. He stands on the deck on all fours and shakes. The salty spray flies all over me.

"Good boy, Kula." I pat his wet fur.

He barks again. And doesn't stop until I paddle back into the waves.

Kula's a lucky dog. He almost died after his rescue. The guy who shot him, a pet thief named Spyder Silva, wasn't so lucky. It's a long story, but the short version is that the retriever was trying to protect Maile—held at gunpoint by Silva. When I saw Kula go down I pulled my Smith & Wesson on Silva. I had to answer to homicide detective Frank Fernandez. Ultimately Fernandez grudgingly agreed I'd acted in self-defense. I was in the clear. But Kula barely hung on. It took months for him to recover. Kula and Maile bonded around that experience. I should be glad she lets me take him surfing. But I'd be gladder if she'd talk to me.

While we wait for another wave I wonder again what I can possibly tell Ransom's daughter, other than I'm sorry for her loss. I wonder even more why she wants to see me.

After Kula and I catch our fill of waves at Flies, I bathe, dry, and return him to Maile's yard. Carrying cousin Alika's tandem board back to her carport, I notice she's home this time. I get bold and pop into her cottage to say thanks.

Maile's three cats curled up on rattan chairs—Coconut, Peppah, and Lolo—barely crane their necks. They know me. Lolo, the shy calico, doesn't even bolt. Scattered about the living room are Kula's toys—rawhide chews, yellow tennis balls, braided tug ropes—and food and water dishes inscribed with his name. He lives like a prince here. *Wish I did, too.*

Maile steps from her bedroom in her Nikes, running shorts, and sports bra. Seeing her tanned limbs and lovely curves again kind of smarts. I remember them too well.

Her face used to light up when she saw me. Not today. She doesn't offer me a chair. I ask how she's doing. We exchange a few terse sentences.

I can see we're getting nowhere fast. I just say goodbye and head for the door. Then she surprises me.

"Too bad about your client at Volcano House," she says with some real feeling.

I turn back. I'd like her to keep talking. "How'd you know he was my client?" I don't remember telling her about Ransom. And my name wasn't in the news reports.

"Tommy," she says. "We were talking about something else and it came up. I was interested because a guy I used to know dated Ransom's wife, Donnie Lam, when he was at Stanford."

"Donnie went to Stanford?" That doesn't sound right.

"No, I don't think so. She was living in the bay area and they met in a bar. He fell hard for her and was broken up when she married some old rich guy."

"You mean Rex Ransom?"

"No. Apparently she was married before. When that husband died she returned to Hawai'i and married Ransom. Or so I heard."

"Really?" Then as an afterthought: "Did Tommy tell you he's getting married again?"

"Yeah." Maile shrugs. "I wished him luck. He'll need it."

"My sentiments exactly." At least we agree on something. So I get even bolder and ask: "How about dinner this week?"

"We'll see," she says noncommittally.

"I'll call you."

I almost float to my car, so pumped up I nearly forget Maile's curious story about Donnie being married before. Almost, but not quite.

She's been widowed by two rich old men?

nineteen

Monday morning that amber haze still hangs over Maunakea Street. I'm waiting for Rex Ransom's daughter. I don't have to wait long.

She's ten minutes early.

When she strides in I recall seeing her at the Kīlauea Camp chapel—she and her dark, statuesque mother looking like a matched set.

"Caitlin Ransom," she says—pleasantly, but businesslike. She offers me her hand. I take it and she shakes mine vigorously. *Shades of her late father?*

She's got to be in her thirties, given her parents' age, but she looks barely twenty-five. Grey eyes. Brown hair trimmed smartly to the shoulders. Little black dress flowing gracefully over her lean frame.

"Kai Cooke," I say. "Won't you have a seat?" I gesture to my client chair.

She sits and adjusts her dress. Her stylish attire and fine features give her that cultivated look young women get in pricey private schools.

"I'm sorry about your father." I say the line I rehearsed in the surf.

"I miss him," she says. "Every day." The mist in her eyes tells me she means it.

"Did you stay in Volcano after Stan Nagahara's funeral?" Since Caitlin vaguely resembles the young woman in red I saw on the trail, I try to make a connection.

"Mother did," she says, "but I had to get back to school in Honolulu. I'm doing graduate work in anthropology."

"So you didn't see or talk to your father the next day—the day he died?"

"Unfortunately not."

"I wish I could have prevented what happened," I start to explain. "You see, Donnie—"

"I'm sure it wasn't your fault." She saves me from rehearsing the lamentable event. "And I'm grateful you agreed to see me."

"So how can I help you?" I ask the question I've been wondering about since her unexpected call.

"My father's death was no accident," Caitlin announces.

"You don't accept the medical examiner's report that he was overcome by fumes?"

She slowly shakes her head. "Dad knew he had a heart condition and he knew the fumes around the volcanoes could be dangerous."

"A woman approached him on the trail moments before he died. I hesitate to say this, but she looked amazingly like one of Pele's well-known guises."

"I know Donnie believes Pele took my father's life," she says. "But I don't."

"Okay, let's say for argument sake you're right. If it wasn't an accident and it wasn't Pele, how did your father end up in the steam vent?"

She trains her grey eyes on me. "That's what I want you to find out."

I don't know why I suddenly feel uncomfortable. I grab for any words I can find—and hope they won't sound flip: "Do you have someone in mind?"

"Maybe Sonny Boy Chang? He assaulted my father two decades ago and has been in and out of prison ever since. He's out now."

"I saw Sonny Boy at the funeral." I recall the bearded, dreadlocked man in camouflage. "If we strike out with him, then who?"

"Lots of people on the Big Island fought geothermal development and disliked my dad." She rattles off a list of essentially the same names that were on my own list. Then she says: "My father sent me a generous check before he died. I'm willing to spend every penny to find out who did this."

"I've got another case going, but I can look into your father's death around it." Then I say, "When the deceased is divorced, like your dad was, it's customary to interview the former spouse. That would be your mother."

"My mother could have nothing to do with this," Caitlin insists.

I remember the nasty scar on her father's right hand, but keep it to myself. "I just want your okay to talk with her."

"You have it." Caitlin gives me her mother's phone number in Kona.

"I should also talk again with your father's second wife," I say. "Did you know she was married once before she met him?"

"I heard her first husband died," Caitlin replies. "Donnie's not my favorite person, as you can imagine, but she doted on my father."

"That was my first impression," I say. Caitlin doesn't need to know my second.

Caitlin Ransom gives me a retainer before she strides from my office. She's hardly out the door when I go on line and book a flight to Hilo for the next morning. I get Pualani at the Volcano House on the phone, we talk story, and I explain why I'm returning so soon. Then I phone Caitlin's mother, Kathryn Ransom, at her Kailua-Kona home and she agrees to see me. Finally I try Ransom's ex-partner Mick London in Kamuela, with a cell number Caitlin provided. He sounds drunk again—*or still?*—but he too agrees. I'm batting one thousand. Except there's no phone number for Pele.

Before I leave the office Monday afternoon, I call Denver again. Neither Ashley nor Ethan answers. I leave more messages—against my own better judgment. I can await their return calls just as well on the Big Island.

Then I phone Tommy Woo. He tells me some jokes too salty to repeat. I ask about his contact with the liquor commission and explain that I need a history of over-serving of customers at the Lollipop Lounge. All Tommy can talk about is Zahra and their wedding plans. I try to change the subject. I ask him about a TRO for Blossom's abusive ex, Junior.

"Worthless," Tommy says. "A TRO may only piss him off more. A piece of paper won't stop a desperate man."

"Mrs. Fujiyama said the same," I say. "Well, sort of."

"She's right." Tommy says. "Best thing your *lei* girl can do is disappear for a while."

Before I lock up for the day I make one final call—to Maile. I get her voicemail. "Hi Maile. It's me. I have to go back to the Big Island for a few days on the Ransom case. When I return I'll give you a call about dinner."

I glide down the shag stairs, feeling almost giddy. But the air comes out of my sails as soon as I see Blossom. I don't have to ask how she's doing. I can tell by the look in her eyes.

"Junior keeps hanging around my apartment," she says. "He keeps driving by the *lei* shop. I don't feel safe anywhere."

I recall Tommy's advice. "I'm going off island for a few days," I say, as the other *lei* girls, Chastity and Joon, look on. "Why don't you stay at my place while I'm gone?" As soon as I say this I realize it's a terrible idea—Tommy's advice, or not.

Blossom perks up. "You sure?"

"I'm sure," I say. But the old saying—*No good deed goes unpunished*—comes to mind. "You can stay tomorrow night. And probably a few nights after that." I explain where I live and how to get into the building. Then I climb back up the stairs and fetch her my extra apartment key.

When I return, Junior's black pickup truck is pulling up in front of the shop. He sees me giving Blossom the key. I make eye contact with him and he flips me the bird. *Again.* Then he lays rubber down Maunakea Street.

"I'm scared." Blossom trembles.

"Come tonight," I hear myself say. "I can walk you through the place so you know what's what." Then it dawns on me that I have a studio apartment with only one bed. "There should be space enough for two," I say, trying to convince myself. *Ah, I'll sleep on the* lānai.

"Oh, *mahalo*, Kai!" She hugs me. *"Mahalo."*

Mrs. Fujiyama—always the protective mother hen— frowns when she sees me lead her *lei* girl out the door. Doesn't she remember I learned the hard way already not to date her girls? Plus this one is nearly half my age.

I glance back at my landlady and shake my head.

twenty

The tiny *lānai* of my studio apartment looks thirty-five stories down into Waikīkī. The only thing between the *lānai* and a very long drop is a thin plate of glass. All night long I listen to traffic below on Ala Wai Boulevard, the chirping tires of racerboys like Fireball, and sirens of HPD cruisers chasing them. Scrunched into a patio chair, hanging in the air above the noisy streets, I dream of Maile's hillside cottage.

My dream is interrupted by Blossom bouncing off my sofa bed, turning on lights, pacing the apartment, and talking on her cell phone. To whom, I don't know. She's in a new place. And maybe she's anxious. I don't blame her, but I also don't get much sleep.

By morning, I'm a wreck. *No good deed goes unpunished.*

After an impromptu breakfast, Blossom and I walk the carpeted hallway to the elevator. One of my neighbors lifts an eyebrow at me when he sees my pretty companion. I drop Blossom at the *lei* shop on my way to the airport. Fortunately, we don't get the same look from Mrs. Fujiyama. I guess by now she's figured it out.

* * *

My plane lands in Hilo at a little before eleven, I pick up a rental car—no wait and no hassles this time, *but sadly no Porsche*—and climb once again to the Volcano House. I pull through the portico of the barn-red hotel, park the car, try not to breathe the sulfur-laden air too deeply, and pass the fireplace on my way to the registration desk. The Park Service sign cautioning about the fumes is still posted.

I don't have to ring the bell.

Pualani greets me with her warm Hawaiian hospitality. She knows why I'm here, but she says playfully, "Kai, why you nevah come back sooner?"

"Was here only las' week," I say. "Remembah?"

She turns to her yellowed keyboard and peers at the monitor that's been around since the dawn of the personal computer. She types on the ancient keys. "Geev you one deluxe crater-view room dis time," she says. *"Kama'aina* rate."

"T'anks, eh?" On my own dime, or should I say on my client's dime, I had reserved the cheapest room in the hotel facing the parking lot rather than the crater.

"Room numbah one," she says. "Da same room da geothermal guy stay in dat wen' *huli* inside da steam vent. Spooky, yeah?"

"Das okay," I say, secretly stoked. I ask Pualani if I can see the guest register for the night before Ransom died. I don't expect to find anything obvious. But maybe a name will pop out. Or maybe a name that means nothing to me now will mean something later.

"I remembah da date," she says. "How I can fo'get?" Her fingers dance on that yellowed keyboard again. When she finds the appropriate record she wrestles the monitor in my direction.

The names on the screen include my own, those of Rex and Donnie Ransom, and the man from Puna Security. The other names don't mean a thing to me.

So I ask Pualani: "Anyt'ing strange happen on dat day?"

"Nah." Then she thinks for a moment. "Wait!" she says. "One guest wen insist fo' crater view room numbah t'ree. He make like big fuss. Said he mus' be on da groun' floor. Afraid of heights. Da hotel full, yeah? But I move da guests suppose to be in numbah t'ree to anoddah room upstairs. He says he come to see da eruption. Den what he do? He check out early da nex' morning—no time to see da eruption."

I glance at the hotel map. Crater view room three sits right next to room one—the Ransoms' room and now my own.

"When he leave da nex' morning?" I ask

"I dunno . . . maybe eight," she replies, which would be before Ransom died.

"What his name?"

She points to it on the screen. Lars Stapleton.

The name doesn't ring a bell. "What dis' guy look like?"

"Small kine *haole* guy," she says.

"Hair color? Eyes?" I try to jog her memory.

"So many people, dey come to da desk," she says. "How I can remembah dem all?"

"Where he from?"

She goes to another screen and scrolls down. "New Jersey."

"Nah." The more I hear about this Stapleton, the more I'm losing interest. His name could be an alias, but his profile doesn't fit any pieces of this puzzle.

"Don' fo'get Pele." Does Pualani want to help—or to pull my leg some more? Here in the park, so close to Pele's home and the mist that surrounds it, how could I forget the legendary goddess or deny her power? Pualani insists: "Pele knows. She da one you need talk to."

"But how I goin' investigate Pele?" I ask like it's a serious question. "How I goin' track down one goddess?"

"I tell you bumbye," she says, by which she means soon enough. Then she winks again.

I walk just a few steps from the registration desk to crater-view room one. This is the biggest view room in the hotel and usually costs double what I'm paying. Not a bad place to cool my heels before the long drive tomorrow to Kona and Waimea, on the other side of the island. Pualani must still like me. Or she's just full of *aloha.*

Though the best room in the house, it's spare like the rest. No TV, no radio, no cable or WīFi. Just a *koa* desk and chair, a small bath with shower, and a closet with a sliding door. There's a beautiful Hawaiian quilt on the double bed. But best of all is the sweeping view of Pele's domain.

I open the windows overlooking the crater, whiff sulfur in the air, and scan smoldering Kīlauea below. Across the desolate expanse, smoke plumes waft lazily into the sky. Despite their slow twirling, beneath them lies a massive unstoppable force— molten magma miles below the surface. And Pele stands for the power behind all this. No wonder so many believe she's a force to be reckoned with.

Turning my gaze away from the windows to the wall against the bed, I see a small door that appears to connect to the next room—crater view room three where guest Lars Stapleton stayed. I unlock the door, not even stopping to think about any guests in the adjoining room who might not welcome my intrusion. The door opens to another identical door.

That door is locked. To enter one room from the other, both doors must be unlocked. Obviously, guests in both rooms must desire and welcome such intimacy.

What this has to do with the death of Rex Ransom, if anything, I don't know. Ransom didn't die in his room. And when I was here with Donnie the door to room three was not open. Lars Stapleton from New Jersey remains off my list of suspects, for now.

At one I walk to the hotel dining room overlooking Kīlauea. It's been less than a week since I watched Rex and Donnie Ransom enjoy their last supper together at a candlelit table. The dining room looks different by daylight. Red oilcloths on the tables glint in the sun. The caldera appears to run for miles. It must be an optical illusion, but it looks like forever. At the far end, nearly out of sight, the smaller but more active Halemaʻumaʻu Crater smolders.

I have my pick of tables, so grab one by a window. Just me and a bottle of Tabasco on the red oilcloth. While I wait for the waitress the image comes to mind of Donnie Ransom walking into the dining room leading her husband by the hand. A picture of devotion. But my cynical side chimes in: *He's loaded and she's half his age.* Then my more charitable side: *If she wanted him dead, why would she hire me to protect him?* But now I wonder again about the secrecy she insisted on. Was it to protect his pride, or to hide that she was having him watched?

I order a Volcano Burger and the waitress leaves me with the view and with my thoughts. When my burger arrives, I pass on the Tabasco and dig in. What Maile said about Donnie pops into my mind. Rex Ransom was not the first rich old man Donnie married. Now she's twice widowed. I look across the caldera and count the steam plumes twirling into the air. I get to twenty-two and stop. I'm procrastinating.

I pay for my burger and step outside onto the Crater Rim Trail. I hike through the tree ferns to The Steaming Bluff. The rotten-egg odor intensifies as I approach the vents. I stop at the exact spot where I found Ransom, lean over the railing, and peer into the gaping hole. It's warmer today and less misty, but the memory of what happened is seared into my mind.

I'm following him, the young woman in red approaches, Donnie calls me and frantically shows me the note, and then I return to find the woman gone and the old man in the vent. Before I dial 911, I survey the scene. I find nothing. No foot-prints, not even Ransom's. The trail reveals zero.

Since it's clearer today and the sun has broken through, I try my search again. I'm sure the guardrails by the vent have been dusted. But the fact that no suspects were pursued sug-gests that no usable prints were found. I go off the trail and explore in a circular, falcon-like pattern, making wider and wider sweeps as I walk in the tall brush. A couple strolls by arm-in-arm, giving me a look. I smile. I'm almost done and still find nothing.

Then I see a glint in the tall brown grass and reach for it. It's lipstick. I remove the cap and crank up the stick. Red.

Fiery red.

twenty-one

Wednesday morning I start early for Kailua-Kona. I take the Belt Road almost due south from Hawai'i Volcanoes National Park to the southern tip of the island—and the south-ern-most point in the United States. It's a craggy stretch with plenty to see—if you like rocks.

The Big Island, as its name implies, is the biggest island in the Hawaiian chain. It has more land area than all the other inhabited islands combined. The drive from Volcano House to the west side's most populous city will take me more than two hours. And the Kona district is not my only stop. From there I'm driving another hour north to Waimea, in the island's northern-most region of Kohala. Adding the return, I'll be on the road the better part of the day.

The long drive gives me time to think. I pull from my aloha shirt the lipstick I found near the steam vent where Ransom died.

Fiery red.

Any hope of usable prints has been dimmed by the lip-stick's exposure to days of mist and sun and rain. Was this the same lipstick worn by the woman who approached Ransom?

Why would she take it along hiking? Maybe to freshen her appearance before meeting a man? An old man?

I slip the lipstick back into my shirt.

Finally come the outskirts of Kailua, the once sleepy fishing village and home of Hawaiian royalty. Kailua and the Kona District have experienced some of the same growing pains as other places in the islands. More building, more traffic, more tourist-oriented development.

I consult my map. Kathryn Ransom lives far from the congestion of Kailua's tourist trade. It wasn't always so busy here. I remember visiting family on the Big Island when I was a *keiki*. I'd fish from the lava rock seawall along Aliʻi Drive, dangling my toes in the crystal-clear water and casting my line into blue Kailua Bay. Just a few hotels lined the shore back then, frequented by *kamaʻaina* and *akamai* travelers who knew about this quiet getaway—a world apart from the bustle of Waikīkī.

I turn off Hawaiʻi Belt Road just outside of town and weave my way into a gated retreat perched above the sea. Her home is hidden behind a grove of areca palms and a green-patina copper gate.

I call on an intercom and get buzzed through. The gate swings open and I edge down a gorgeous flagstone drive. More palms—stately Royals—line either side. At the end is an estate rambling over several prime oceanfront acres. I park under a granite-columned porte-cochere by a carriage house. I step out to the sound of pounding surf. *She did well in her divorce.*

I follow more flagstones to sea-blue stained glass doors and knock. Soon the statuesque woman I'd seen at the funeral appears. Kathryn Ransom smiles. Her shoulder-length brown hair is no less meticulously arranged than on the day of the funeral and, though silver-flecked, reminds me of Caitlin.

"Thank you for seeing me on such short notice, Mrs. Ransom," I say. "I'm very grateful."

"Please call me Kathryn," she says in a voice as lovely as her daughter's and leads me in. Up close, she's just as elegant as I remember. She's in cream today, rather than black, and it sets off her coloring nicely. I guess her age in the sixties—about twenty years older than Rex Ransom's second wife.

Kathryn Ransom's home looks way too big for one person; clearly it was the family residence before the divorce. As we walk there's a glimpse, on the right, into a spacious kitchen of oak and granite and stainless steel. A knife rack above one of the stone countertops glints with what looks like pricey German blades.

We pass into a magnificent living room overlooking the sea. The golden bamboo floor glows in the streaming sunlight. We sit on a white leather sofa, almost as immense as the white grand piano across from it. Lettering on the piano says STEINWAY & SONS.

Tommy would drool.

I start things off easy by gesturing to the piano. "That's a beautiful instrument."

"It's a concert grand," she says. "We bought it at the New York factory and had it shipped here." She pauses. "Do you like music?"

"I do. Would you play something for me?" I don't know why I say this. It just pops out.

Kathryn Ransom's face glows. "Yes, of course. What would you like to hear?"

"Maybe one of your favorites?"

"Okay." She rises and walks to the piano, sits, and lifts the fallboard covering the keys. Her profile at the white piano is silhouetted against the blue sea. She settles herself, takes a breath, and says, "This is a calm, contemplative little piece. It helped me through the divorce."

"What's it called?"

"'Gymnopédie' by Eric Satie." She pronounces it *zhim-no-PAY-dee*. And it might as well be Greek, because I have no idea what it means. Then she says, "Satie was French." So I know I'm way off.

She starts to play—slowly and softly. The tune is simple, serene, and haunting. Her fingers move gracefully over the keys. The piano sounds bell-like and brilliant. I can't believe I'm hearing concert hall music in a private home in Kailua-Kona. The melody calms me, yet makes me yearn. I know I've heard it before, but don't remember where or when.

As the serene tune continues I wonder what an equally serene world would be like—a world in perfect harmony. And while I know that's not possible, the piece puts me in a space where I can imagine it. Everything is ordered and beautiful. Everyone loves and cares. All work for peace and the common good. Nobody gets divorced. Nobody steals. Nobody cheats and lies. Nobody murders.

My reverie continues as long as the piece does—just a few precious minutes. When it's over, my hands feel damp.

She turns to me. "Did you like it?"

When she asks this I suddenly recall her ex-husband's limo driver saying, "She wen stab 'em, brah!" I can't picture it. *These graceful hands wielding a knife?* Then I remember her eyes turning blank at the funeral when she saw her ex with his second wife. *No love lost.*

A strained look now crosses Kathryn Ransom's face. Finally I choke out, "That was beautiful. You're very good."

"Thank you." She seems relieved. "Satie wrote two more variations. But I'll spare you for now."

With the musical prelude over, I start my questions. "Would you mind telling me about the time your husband checked into Hilo Hospital with a knife wound? I can't imagine you had anything to do with it. You just don't seem like the kind of person . . ."

Her eyes go blank—like at the funeral. I sit quietly and wait.

She doesn't speak. She turns back to the piano and starts to play again. The musical prelude is *not* over. The piece sounds like rippling water. It's beautiful. I'm entranced, by both the tune and her refusal to talk. I almost don't care. The melody carries me away.

When it ends she says, "That's Bach's 'Prelude in C'. So simple. So exquisite. Another little piece that helped me through the divorce."

I nod and wait.

She finally starts to talk. "Kai, I wasn't myself during the divorce. I was self-medicating to get through it—if you know what I mean."

I nod again. That's a euphemistic way of saying she was blasted.

"I just sort of snapped. I'd given him everything for thirty years. I gave him three children. I followed him everywhere—from one drilling site to another around the world. I was devoted and loyal and loving. And—with him—that wasn't always easy."

"I understand." I let her keep going.

"But when he lied to me . . . when he deceived me . . . when he took up with that woman half his age behind my back." She pauses. "I'm not proud of what I did. At that moment, I wanted him dead."

"Do you mind if I ask you where you were on the morning your ex-husband did die?" I wonder if she's going to start playing again. She doesn't.

"I was driving from Volcano back to Kona. I stayed overnight with Stan Nagahara's wife. We've always been close and she wanted me with her after the service."

"Do you remember what time you drove?"

"Not exactly. I ate breakfast first with Kyoko. Maybe nine or nine-thirty?"

"Anyone ride with you?"

"Just me. Caitlin flew back to Honolulu. She had classes at the University."

"When did you learn of your ex-husband's death?"

"Oh, it wasn't until that night. Nobody official called me, of course. I'm not his wife anymore. I saw it on the TV news. Caitlin hadn't heard, nor her brothers on the mainland. I had to tell them."

"I'm sorry," I say.

"When the divorce was over, I just wanted to put him behind me. But my children still needed him. And he wasn't there. I'm sorry for them. Before he died they were just getting close to him again after a long estrangement. Why would I kill him? He was finally coming to his senses and considering his own family."

I shift gears. "Are you still in touch with Mr. Ransom's ex-partner, Mick London? I'm going to see him this afternoon. Anything you can tell me about him might help."

"Mick lost everything when Rex pulled out of Puna. I talked with him about six months ago. He's living in a tiny shack and drives an old beat up truck.

"I saw the truck," I say, "at the funeral."

"His belated entrance was hard to miss." Kathryn shakes her head. "From what I've heard, Mick ekes out a meager existence by scavenging scrap metal. Other than that, he just drinks and fishes. If he didn't fish, he wouldn't eat. This is a man who was once very successful. But when the company failed he discovered he was too old to start over. He blames Rex entirely."

"He's bitter about losing his business?"

"That's only half of it. Mick was dating Donnie Lam before she married Rex. She was some kind of PR person the company hired. She was already widowed, from what I heard. Then she latched onto my husband. I'm not much for women who do things like that."

I pull the lipstick I found on the Crater Rim Trail from my pocket and crank it open. "Does this look familiar?"

She studies its fiery red hue. "No. Should it?"

"Is it a color that you or, say, your daughter might wear? Or anybody you know?"

"I doubt it," she says. "Well, maybe Rex's second wife. That looks like her style. Where did you find it?"

I fudge. "Somebody dropped it and I picked it up."

We talk a while longer. What I finally take away from the interview is that Kathryn Ransom admits to stabbing her husband during their acrimonious divorce. She also admits to being in or around Volcano on the morning her husband died. She has no alibi as to her exact whereabouts. She says she was driving back to Kona alone. She had the opportunity to kill her husband. But to hear her talk now, not the motive. She claims she's over the divorce and over her late ex-husband. And I can't link her, at this point, to the young woman in red.

I find myself believing Kathryn Ransom. For now.

twenty-two

It's after one when the green copper gate at Kathryn Ransom's oceanfront estate closes behind me. I make tracks for Waimea.

The highway north of Kailua along the Kohala Coast looks like a bomb went off. From the mountains to the sea, the roadside is charred and empty. It wasn't a bomb that did this. It was a volcano. Hualālai, the island's third most active. The lack of rain in this arid region doesn't help recovery. The lava flow looks like it happened just yesterday, not two hundred years ago. The only things that seem to sprout in the blackness are the luxury oceanfront resorts at Waikoloa and the cryptic white coral graffiti along the highway: "Shade Dada," "Thelma + Louise," and "sadkids.com." And the not so cryptic: "Aloha, Mom," "Suck it up," and "Jess loves Bryan." Or is it "Jeff loves Byron"?

I pass the sprawling resorts along the shore and then climb northeast into the ranchlands of Waimea, officially called Kamuela. The air cools and the roadside greens. This is the high country of Parker Ranch—famous for its fine beef cattle—where verdant pasturelands roll gently from snow-capped Mauna Kea toward the sparkling blue sea.

Kathryn Ransom wasn't exaggerating when she said Mick London lives in a shack. An abandoned utility shed, really. Weathered grey boards. Rusty tin roof. One window and one door. Next to the shed is his beat-up truck. The bed is heaped with scrap metal. And one fishing pole. The faded letters on the door—LONDON DRILLING EQUIPMENT—make little sense now.

The shed's door doesn't have a knob. Only a hasp and padlock. The lock is open. The key in. I assume that means Mick is home. I knock on a grey board, my knuckles managing to avoid splinters.

"Jus' a min—" drawls a slurred voice from behind the boards.

I wait. Crashing sounds make me think I've come at a bad time. I check my watch. It's a little after two.

The door finally creaks open, revealing the white-bearded Father Time I saw at the funeral. Mick London is hunched over and smells like a barroom. His flushed face suggests too much whiskey and too much Hawaiian sun. And his murky eyes more of the same. The grime on his tattered shirt and holey jeans reminds me of the Chinatown winos who hang out by Mrs. Fujiyama's dumpster.

The shack smells like he does. A half empty whiskey bottle sits on the dirt floor by his unmade cot. He motions me to sit in the only chair in the place. He stumbles to his cot.

"Wan' some?" He reaches for the whiskey.

I shake my head. "I'm good."

"Doan mine if I do." He takes a swig.

I thank him for seeing me on short notice. Then I start off friendly and easy. I ask him where he fishes.

"Fissssh?" he looks surprised. "Near Mauna Kea Resor'," he manages to say. "On the rocks."

"What do you catch?"

"Ulua," he replies.

"Really?" *Ulua* is a large, white-meat game fish, prized by local fishermen.

"Yeahhh." He takes another drink. "Fur dinner." Fish seems to be, as Kathryn Ransom said, his only sustenance. Besides whisky.

I ask him how he teamed up with Rex Ransom.

"Tha' *sonofabitch!*" Mick reddens. "We go *waaay* back." Mick says he came with Ransom Geothermal from Montana to be Rex's plant manager in Puna. But then he started a side business with his boss's blessing and sold his wares exclusively to him. It was a great deal for Ransom, I gather, since Mick took the risks of acquiring and stocking the equipment. He admits he made good money while the arrangement lasted, but was not prepared—not even told—when Ransom abruptly pulled out of Puna. Mick eventually filed for bankruptcy.

"Did Ransom help you in any way?" I ask.

"Tha' *sonofabitch?*" Mick is about to boil. He explains he took Ransom to court, but the CEO's shifty lawyers prevailed.

"Too bad," I say, trying to keep him going.

"An' tha' *bitsch* he marry—" Mick spits out the words. "She wuz gonna marry meee!"

"Donnie?" It sounds unlikely.

"Yeahhh, tha' *shlutt!*" Mick goes on to say that when Donnie sniffed what was coming—his bankruptcy—she jumped ship.

"Make you angry to see them together at the funeral?" I ask.

Mick's face reddens. He gawks at me.

He's right. It was a stupid question.

"Dey deserff eash other!" He sneers. "Doze two!" Mick claims Donnie only married Ransom for his money. Which gives her a good reason to want him dead. "If Pele didn' keeel 'em," Mick says, "Donnie did!"

"How could Donnie kill Rex?" I ask. "I was with her when he died."

"Jus' kiddin'," Mick says. "Sour grapes."

I shrug. "Do you mind if I ask where you were when he died, the Wednesday after the funeral?"

"Doan remember," he says. And I believe him. He was smashed.

"Did you drive home after the service? Did you stay another night in Volcano?"

Mick looks puzzled. "Now I remember—I drove but I got shleepy. I pulled off an' shlept."

"Where?" He obviously couldn't see straight.

"I dunno."

"Did you get a room?"

"Nah. Wadda I wan' a room fur? Got my truck."

"Did you see or talk to anyone?"

He shakes his head. He's got no alibi. He seems to know that. But I've got no evidence against him. He seems to know that too.

We talk more. I ask more questions. Time passes.

"Thanks," I finally say. "Gotta long drive back to Volcano."

He nods and I stand. Mick rolls back on his cot and hoists his whiskey. "To yo' healff."

I let myself out and soon begin winding down the Hamakua Coast, mulling over the interview. *Opportunity.* Mick London has no alibi on the morning Ransom died. *Motive.* He's still bitter about his old boss taking away his livelihood and, Mick claims, his woman. *Means.* But how could he do it? Even if he showed up on the Crater Rim Trail that fateful morning, Mick was in no condition to kill a flea. And what possible connection could he have to the young woman in red?

* * *

Back at the Volcano House Wednesday evening I get a call from Tommy Woo. He tells his obligatory jokes and then asks, "Whatever happened to your little *lei* girl and her thug boyfriend?"

"Blossom may be little, Tommy. But she's not a girl. She's twenty. If you want to know, she's staying in my apartment while I'm on the Big Island."

"*Bad* idea," he says.

I know he's right, but I say, "You yourself advised she should disappear for a while."

Tommy shrugs it off. "What are you doing back on the Big Island?"

"Didn't I tell you? Ransom's daughter hired me to look into his death. She doesn't believe an accident put him in that steam vent."

"You're investigating *Pele?*" Tommy's tone suggests he's ribbing me.

"Yeah," I respond in kind. "I've got her on the ropes. I'll have a complete confession before I leave. Guaranteed." Then I go him one better. "And if the goddess refuses to confess, there's a few human suspects I like for the crime."

"Good man . . ." Tommy pauses. "But you better be careful about lending your apartment to the *lei* girl. When her ex-boyfriend finds out, he's gonna think you're her new guy."

"His name's Junior and he already thinks that. He's wrong."

There's a beep on my cell phone indicating an incoming call. I glance at caller ID. *Maile?* No. Area code 303. *Denver.* The Pali case. *I've got to take this call!* But just as I tell Tommy to hang on, the number disappears.

"*Sh—!*" I say.

"What's wrong?" Tommy asks.

"I got another call, from Denver—probably the Lindquist twins' friend who may be the key to the Pail case. I've been waiting on her for a week."

"She'll leave a message," Tommy says. "Anyway, you better watch your back for this Junior dude. I bet he's got a rap sheet as long as his arm."

"And outstanding warrants," I say. "He's gonna do some time, once HPD gets him off the street."

Then Tommy coyly asks, "Remember what I told you about Zahra?"

At first I draw a blank. "Oh, yeah. You're going to ask Zahra to marry you."

"Right," he explains. "Otherwise she has to go back to Kenya."

My phone beeps again—this time with the tone indicating a new voicemail. *From Denver?*

"Sounds like you've got it all figured out." I'm getting impatient because I've already reminded him about his two marriages. After the second he got his cats, Miles and Charlie, and swore off marriage forever. Truth is, Tommy isn't cracked up to be a husband. His late-night gigs after long days at his office mean he's seldom home. I'm surprised his cats haven't left him.

"I've got to pull the trigger soon," Tommy continues. "I've got to co-sign that fiancé visa, or she has to go back."

"Tommy, you already have my blessing. Whatever makes you happy, my friend."

"Well, I have a favor to ask you about the wedding." He pauses and I wonder what's coming. "Would you be my best man?"

"Do I have to wear a tux?" I'm looking for a way out. I'm not much for weddings, or any kind of formal events. Sunset on the beach with a few beers. That's my kind of celebration.

"Nah," Tommy replies. "Zahra and I are wearing African wedding robes. You can wear whatever you like."

"Swell," I say. "I'll be there."

"T'anks, eh?" Tommy hangs up.

I call my voicemail and retrieve my new message.

"Hi, this is Ashley," says the twenty-something female voice. "I'm totally sorry I haven't called you back. I like left my cell phone on the airplane, you know?"

Is she asking me or telling me?

"It took the airline a really long to find it! *Bogus.*"

Bogus?

"Whatever," Ashley continues. "I'm flying back tomorrow—okay?—and can meet you Friday, like at noon. I work at Safari in Ala Moana Shopping Center. For sure I'll bring my pics of Heather and Lindsay's twenty-first birthday party. *Way* sad."

Then she says as an afterthought. "Oh, Ethan got your messages. He's like just a guy I know in Denver. He wasn't at the twins' party."

Okay, Ethan wasn't at the twins' party. But why was his phone number riding with them in Fireball's car?

I save Ashley's message. Now I have another question to ask her on Friday.

twenty-three

Thursday morning I stop by the desk at the Volcano House and ask Pualani if she has any idea where I might find Ikaika "Sonny Boy" Chang. It's a big island—but not that big. Like most island communities, this one is tight.

Hearing Sonny Boy's name seems to startle her. She composes herself and then says that after the Save Pele Coalition disowned him for dragging Ransom from his car, Sonny Boy has been in and out of prison, but recently returned on parole to Volcano, where he lives only about a mile away. She claims he's a new man. *We'll see.*

"Sonny Boy stay only one mile from da Volcano House? You got one address fo' 'em?"

"No need address," she says. "Volcano one small kine village, yeah?" She tells me how to find his digs. "But he no *make* da geothermal guy. I know. Pele da one."

"How you know he no do 'em?"

"Jus' know." She gets a tortured look on her face. "Sonny Boy at home," she says.

I wonder how she knows. "You okay?" I ask.

She nods, but her eyes tell a different story. Leaving the desk I ponder what just happened and what Pualani has to do with Sonny Boy.

* * *

I drive Hilo-bound on Highway 11, from the main gate of Hawai'i Volcanoes National Park to Volcano Village. The journey downslope is barely one mile.

In less than a minute I turn off the highway into Volcano Village. The village's scattered homes and B&Bs spread over several miles of high rainforest at the cool elevation of nearly four thousand feet. Its post office and dozen or so small businesses—restaurants, hardware store, and two general stores—all straddle Old Volcano Road, once the main highway around the island. Frequent rains keep everything in Volcano green and mossy.

The old highway that connects the village's main streets is damp. It's not raining now, but the next shower is always coming. Only a few thousand people live here. The village gives off a hang-loose-aging-hippie vibe. It's a place where independent-minded artists, crafts- and trade-persons, retirees, wilted flower children, and corporate dropouts end up after long years of playing the game. Not the mention lifelong residents who are none of the above.

How Sonny Boy fits into this vibe, I don't know. He certainly wasn't hang-loose when he dragged Ransom from his car some two decades ago. I recall the CEO's limo driver, Kawika, saying Sonny Boy grew *pakalolo* back then on the land cleared for drilling. Maybe protecting his crop made his protest turn violent? When I asked why Chang had attended

Stan Nagahara's funeral, Kawika said the former protester was probably just glad to see Nagahara dead. And would also be glad to see Ransom dead.

No surprise Caitlin named Sonny Boy her suspect number one.

Off the old highway sits a plantation-style cottage on an overgrown jungle that's seen better days. I pull in. That's not where Sonny Boy lives. He lives down an equally overgrown path that weaves out of sight behind the cottage. I drive down the path, just wide enough for one car, into a clearing. Sitting on blocks is a rust-orange shipping container, the kind you see on Matson ships, with a window cut in at one end and a door at the other.

I knock on the rusty metal door. I expect it to open to the sweet-sour odor of *pakalolo*. No. The container smells like wild ginger. Has he kicked the habit?

He steps toward me. He's not a big man, but wiry and muscular.

"Ikaika?" I say. "I'm Kai. Pualani say maybe you like talk wit' me?"

"Shoots," he says, "Call me Sonny Boy." He shows me in.

The ginger scent intensifies as I follow him. Then I see why. In one corner a plastic bucket that says LONDON DRILLING EQUIPMENT—a relic of his protesting days?—brims with the yellow ginger that grows along the highway.

"You know Pualani long?" I ask and check him out more closely.

Mop of brown hair. Sun-bleached dreadlocks. Dark, intense eyes—with the martyr look in those biblical illustrations of Jesus. But Sonny Boy's eyes are fiercer.

"Pualani no tell you?" His fierce eyes warm.

"No tell me what?" I say.

"I'm Malia's daddy."

Whose daddy? Then it dawns on me. *Pualani's tortured look. Her teenage girl.*

"Shoots," I say. Sonny Boy and Pualani must have hung out together during the protests. Then on one of his return trips from prison, I guess, Pualani had his baby.

"You surprise?" he asks. "Das why I here in Volcano. To be wit' Malia."

I shrug and look around the rusty container. On the plank floor sits a small bookshelf with volumes on Hawaiian history and law. And a photo of a smiling teenager who looks like Pualani. No TV. No electricity, I guess. There's one short stool and a sagging single bed against one metal wall and a surfboard against the other. That's it.

I try to connect with him. "Where you surf, brah?"

"Pohoiki in Lower Puna." Sonny Boy gestures to the stool. I plant myself on it and he sits cross-legged on the floor. "Da bes', brah. But when I can go surfing? No wheels."

"Maybe we go togeddah sometime," I say. "I got one car hea, but no board."

He perks up. Regardless of what I've heard about him, I'm starting to like Sonny Boy. His daughter is his life. He surfs. Maybe he is a changed man?

"What you t'ink 'bout da guy Rex Ransom wen' *huli* in da steam vent?" I ask.

Sonny Boy's eyes turn fierce again. "Good riddance. He deserve 'em. He rip up da rainforest and he rape Pele."

"You like tell me, brah, you hea when he wen' *huli?*"

"Wuz hea in Volcano," Sonny Boy says. "Pele did 'em. Case close. When I pull da guy outta his car, I do 'em fo' Pele. She acting t'rough me."

"Maybe Pele act t'rough again?"

"Nah," Sonny Boy says. "Dis time she no need me, or any-body." He looks me in the eyes. "No mo' jail again fo' dat guy. *Nevah.* I stay wit' Malia."

Sonny Boy didn't get off lightly. Most men in Ransom's position, for PR sake, would have let an incident like this go. But he pressed charges, attended court hearings, and spoke out against Chang at every opportunity. Why wouldn't Sonny Boy carry a grudge? Not to mention that he seems to think his actions were divinely inspired.

"Why I *make* Ransom?" he continues. "No need. Pele do 'em. All t'ree dead now. Firs' da plant manager. Den da attor-ney. And now da beeg boss. It more den one coincidence. Don't you t'ink, brah?"

"Could be," I say. And I wonder: *Would he risk parole to take another hack at Ransom? Would he risk being with his daughter?*

"If you don't believe me," Sonny Boy says, "ask Pele's sis-tah, Hi'iaka. She see da whole t'ing."

"She see Pele kill Ransom? Da crazy woman? Da escape mental patient?"

"Sure t'ing, brah. Go ask her yourself."

"Where I fine' her?"

"Secret place," Sonny Boy says. "You got one car?"

I nod. "Told you awready, brah."

"I take you, den," he says.

twenty-four

Sonny Boy and I climb into my car. He's carrying a plastic shopping bag half filled with papayas and apple-bananas. We start to roll and he says, "You like take one *makana,* one gift, to Hiʻiaka?"

"What *kine* gift?" I ask.

"One bottle of gin," Sonny Boy says. "An' one pack of Camels." He tells me Hiʻiaka should be honored in the same way her sister Pele is honored.

"Fo' sure?" I'm thinking this is a scam. I'm thinking the gin and Camels will end up in Sonny Boy's hands.

He nods. He's not kidding.

Sonny Boy directs me to a little general store on the Old Volcano Highway. It's one of those tiny, all-purpose marts where villagers can get everything they need without having to drive to Hilo. The fifth of gin and pack of Camels sets me back nearly twenty-five bucks. I pocket the receipt, wondering how to justify this expense to my client.

We climb into the car again and head into the park. I take Crater Rim Drive past the Volcano House and start to circle the three-mile Kīlauea Caldera. Sonny Boy is not saying where we're going.

So I ask, "How you know da goddess?"

"Hiʻiaka?" he asks.

"Yeah, Hiʻiaka—Serena Barrymore."

"From da protess'," he says. "Not name Serena anymo'. Dat was befor' da protess'. We protess' togeddah da drilling in da rainforest."

"You know da guy she *make*, da guy she push in front da bus?"

"Nevah know da guy. Was in prison den."

I nod and keep driving. The caldera stays on our left as we continue along the counterclockwise circle. It's mid-morning and The Steaming Bluff, where Ransom died, raises a thin mist into the sapphire sky. The odor of sulfur seeps into the car, despite closed windows.

I turn to Sonny Boy. "Where we going?"

He nods in a forward direction.

I keep my eyes on the road ahead. We pass the Kīlauea Military Camp, site of Stan Nagahara's funeral, and then the Jaggar Museum and the Southwest Rift Overlook.

Sonny Boy's face looks confident, even amused. He's got a secret. And he knows I want it. But at least he seems to be cooperating with me. Or is he leading me into some remote, quiet place where I could easily disappear?

Soon we approach Halemaʻumaʻu Crater, where Karl Kroften's crushed BMW was found.

I shrug. "Here? Where Pele live?"

Sonny Boy gazes ahead and grins, like the cat that ate the bird. He's enjoying himself. He likes to keep me wondering.

We swing around the bottom of the circle, where Crater Rim Drive carves into lava flows of the 1970s and 1980s. As long ago as that was, the roadside still looks charred. Only a few sprigs of green sprout from cracks in the black rock.

We pass Devastation Trail—a winding path into a scorched forest. Then Thurston Lava Tube, a tunnel as big around as an airliner that was formed by a river of molten lava. Sonny Boy raises his brows and says, "Almos'."

I drive by the Thurston Tube. About a half-mile later he says, "Pull ovah."

I do and we climb out. He grabs his shopping bag with papayas and bananas and I grab my gin and smokes. We walk back toward the lava tube.

"Where we goin', brah?" I ask.

"I show you." He keeps walking.

We walk in single file along the shoulder of the road. Soon Sonny Boy steps through a break in a fern hedge and we find ourselves on a trail that weaves through a forest. The air is moist and cool. An invisible stream gurgles. A chorus of crickets and birds serenades us.

"Dis where Hiʻiaka live?" I ask. "On dis trail?"

"In one secret lava tube, brah," Sonny Boy says.

I consider what he's said. The Thurston Tube is the most famous, but there are hundreds in the park and in the East Rift Zone where lava flows to the sea. Some tubes have been charted and explored, by the likes of Stan Nagahara who died in one, but others remain mysteries.

Sonny Boy leads the way. The trail gets narrower and the forest thicker. This would be a perfect place to rub out a PI who's too *niele*—too nosey. If the ex-con has anything to do with Rex Ransom's death, or the deaths of his two officers under equally suspicious circumstances, he could disappear me here—if not forever, for a very long time. I size up Sonny Boy again and decide to take my chances.

"We there yet?" I'm already breaking into a sweat. The sun is blazing, we're hiking up and down and around, and there's not much air among the giant ferns.

"Almos'," he says again.

And, true to his word, not one minute later he slows down, stops, and scans the trail as if he's searching for something. He looks and looks and then says: "Hea." Meaning, this is the place.

He squeezes through some more tree ferns into one of those hidden, uncharted lava tubes. While the Thurston Tube is lighted for the convenience and safety of park visitors, this tube is dark.

We head in. We've got no flashlight. But Sonny Boy lights a match. We can see again. The tube starts off barely high enough to stand, then gets smaller. We duck our heads. The floor is rough and uneven. Sonny Boy lights another match.

I'm smelling sulfur again. The tube narrows. I see a dim light ahead. And then I smell fresh air.

"Almos' dere," Sonny Boy says.

Finally we step into full light. And a fairy tale.

A rainbow arches over a grove of 'ōhi'a and a gently rolling stream. Brilliant red birds, 'I'iwi, the Hawaiian honeycreeper, hover over the colorful lehua blooms. Everything is green and dewy and luminous in the sun. It looks like an enchanted rainforest. *Unreal.*

"Dis where da goddess stay," he says. He points in the direction of the rainbow.

Under the resplendent arch above that 'ōhi'a grove a barebreasted woman dances the *hula.*

"Das her?"

Sonny Boy nods.

twenty-five

She's wearing a red *haku lei* on her grey head and a ti-leaf skirt. Another red *lei* hangs around her neck, resting on her breasts. She's not ample like Hawaiian goddesses of legend. I can count her ribs as she dances the *hula*—her hips swaying, her arms undulating, her hands in gentle fluid motion. Her eyes are closed and she chants as she moves.

Sonny Boy puts a finger to his lips. "*Ssssshh,*" he says.

Quietly we come closer. Barrymore's red *lei* are *lehua* flowers from the *'ōhi'a* tree. The tree she killed for.

She stands on a mossy perch above us, her delicate *lei* contrasting with her leathery skin. Neither her complexion nor her features look Hawaiian. Nearly three decades ago she threatened Ransom and accused him of raping her sister and of desecrating her rainforest. Back then, Barrymore was considered crazy, but harmless. That was before she committed second-degree murder. If she could push a man into the path of a bus, she could push Ransom into a steam vent.

An escaped mental patient can't make it long on the outside without help. *Sonny Boy.* Why is he helping her? Did they conspire to kill Ransom?

Her eyes suddenly open and she peers down on us.

"I am Pele's favorite sister, Hi'iaka, patron of *hula* and protector of trees and ferns and rainforests." She speaks slowly and distantly, like she's in a trance. "I bring new life and heal the land after Pele's lava flows. I was conceived in Tahiti, daughter of Haumea and Kāne. My beloved sister carried me to Hawai'i cradled in her bosom."

"Hi'iaka, it's me," Sonny Boy says. "I bring you one *makana,* one gift."

She perks up when she hears the word *makana.* Sonny Boy hands her the papayas and apple-bananas. She takes them.

"Dis Kai." He gestures to me. "Kai bring one *makana* too."

I hand her the gin and cigarettes. She sets them on her mossy perch next to Sonny Boy's gift.

"Kai like talk wit' you," he says.

She smiles eerily, which I guess means, "Okay."

I start to ask a question, but get distracted by her breasts. I'm not used to seeing women unclothed in broad daylight. I try to keep my eyes on her face. Some words finally tumble out: "Beautiful *hula*—beautiful forest."

"This is my *'ōhi'a* grove," she says in perfect English. "The *'ōhi'a* is sacred to me. I am its protector."

"To cut them down is a sacrilege," I say. "Just like drilling in the Wao Kele O Puna rainforest. Do you remember the drilling?"

"Hi'iaka never forgets," she says.

"And the protests in the rainforest against the man you called 'the evil one'?"

"He deserved death at Pele's hands," she says.

"Not death at *your* hands?"

"Pele took her own revenge. I saw with my own eyes."

"You saw Pele pitch him into the steam vent?"

"Yes, I saw."

This conversation is getting loonier by the minute. But I'm beginning to wonder who's loonier: her for telling me this wacky stuff, or me for asking questions that prompt it.

"Okay, Goddess Hiʻiaka." I play along. "Tell me what you saw."

"Pele was in her most provocative *kinolau*—flowing red dress, shimmering long hair, vivid eyes, and lips as fiery as a lava flow."

Barrymore didn't have to see the woman on the trail to get these details. This guise is legendary. I'm not convinced.

I turn to Sonny Boy, who's taking it all in.

"It da truth," he says. "The goddess nevah lie."

She continues: "The old man—the evil one—saw Pele coming and tried to run. But he fell to the ground, gasping for air."

Was that the thud and groan I heard? I wonder. But I reply, "How did he get into the vent?"

"Pele," she says again. "Then she ran down the trail past me."

"You're sure you saw her?"

"I'm sure because she dropped something."

"What?" I ask, expecting more nonsense.

"The lipstick that makes her lips fiery red."

"Can't be." The words slip out.

"I held the lipstick in my own hands," Barrymore insists. "Then I left it along the trail, in case my sister came back for it. She didn't. She kept running."

From my pocket I pull the lipstick. "Did it look like this?"

"Yes," Barrymore says. "Just like that."

Sonny Boy turns to me. "Believe now?"

twenty-six

We make our return trip through the dark tunnel. My skeptical side is protesting. I almost believe the young woman I saw on the trail—the same woman Serena Barrymore says she saw—was a *kinolau* of Pele. Almost. I air my doubts.

"Madame Pele immortal, yeah?" I ask Sonny Boy.

"Das right," he replies.

"Den why she need one mortal lipstick? Why not she jus' make her lips any kine color she want?"

"Dunno, brah," answers Sonny Boy. "Pele do whatevah she want. If she want one mortal lipstick, she do 'em."

"Or maybe Goddess Hi'iaka jus' dress up like Pele? Maybe Hi'iaka herself pitch Ransom inside da vent?"

"Don't t'ink so, brah," he says. "Hi'iaka too old. Maybe she can pitch 'em inside da vent, but she no can look like one young *wahine*."

Sonny Boy has a point. The woman I saw was definitely young. Serena Barrymore could not have resembled that woman, even in the mist. As we emerge from the tube into daylight and walk back to the car, I realize my investigation so far has turned up more evidence implicating Pele than any human suspect. That's fine—if you believe in goddesses.

For the sake of thoroughness, I have Sonny Boy write in my spiral notebook his recollection of Barrymore's story, signed and dated—the loony tale of a crazy woman verified by an ex-con on parole. *Solid evidence?* The best I've got.

*   *   *

Back at the Volcano House I grab a sandwich in the hotel dining room. After lunch I'm walking by the reception desk where Pualani has just been extending her *aloha* to a hotel guest.

"Eh, Kai," Pualani says, "So you meet da *lolo wahine* dat t'ink she one goddess?"

"How'd you know?" I ask, before I put two and two together and come up with the inevitable: Sonny Boy.

"Jus' know." Pualani says again. "She no mo' Goddess Hi'iaka den dis bell on da desk." *Ding!—Ding!* Pualani rings the little chrome bell for effect. "She *lolo.* Da *wahine* sick."

I agree with her. "She say she see Pele, in da *kinolau* of one beautiful young *wahine*, pitch da geothermal boss inside da vent. You evah see one woman like dat 'round hea?"

"I no see her," she says, "but was Pele. She *make* da oddah two. Why not da boss? Pele your suspect numbah one!"

"You t'ink so?"

"Fo' sure. You gotta go to Halema'uma'u Crater at sunset wit' 'ōhelo berries. Make her one offering. She come to you. Guarantee."

I slowly nod.

But, Pualani warns me, it's not the best time to visit the crater. Its floor—the thin crust resting on a lake of boiling lava—is bulging. Park volcanologists worry another eruption is coming. She describes fiery fountains spewing ash and molten rock into the air. She cautions me to be careful.

"T'anks, eh?" I think of the cliché: *fool's errand.* Then I go it one better: *dangerous fool's errand.*

Back in my room I catch up on paperwork. I write out detailed notes about my four interviews on the Big Island with Kathryn Ransom, Mick London, Ikaika "Sonny Boy" Chang, and Serena Barrymore, a.k.a. Goddess Hiʻiaka. I will refer to these notes when I report back to my client. I can't count out any of these four suspects just yet. But while all four had, to varying degrees, motive, opportunity, and means to kill Rex Ransom, the interviews lead me to believe none actually did kill him. Unless one of the four incriminates him- or herself, or unless another suspect surfaces, I'm left with only *Pele.*

Barrymore claims she saw the goddess heave Ransom into the vent. I can dismiss her description of Pele's widely-known *kinolau,* but not the lipstick I later recovered on the trail. Barrymore had to be there for that. And so I'm stuck with her story. Stuck at least with part of it. To believe it all, I'd have to believe that the goddess materialized bodily on this earth and caused the death of a mortal man.

That's a huge leap.

I lie back on the bed and decide that it might not be a bad idea to at least check in with Pele later at the Halemaʻumaʻu Crater. Maybe it could help me get into a frame of mind to understand how so many people, some of them at least apparently sane, could conclude that it had to be the goddess who pushed the old man to his death.

I'm not a normally a napper, but the long drive yesterday and fitful sleep last night make me drift off.

Suddenly I'm on the edge of the crater at sunset gazing into the fiery pit. Standing over the hiss and roar, I wait for the goddess to appear. Finally she does. Pele rises out of the flames as the seductive young woman I saw on the trail. She says my name and promises to tell me everything. Before she does I awake.

It's late afternoon—little time to spare before sunset. I drag myself out to gather an offering for Pele. Yes, I actually do this.

I don't have to hike far on the Crater Rim Trail. Just to The Steaming Bluff. Sulfur fills the air. By the vent where I found the old man I spot the green-leafed stems of the ʻōhelo plant reaching skyward and carrying pale yellow to bright red clusters of fruit, about the size of blueberries. There's plenty to choose from. The *nene,* or Hawaiian goose, loves these berries and disperses their seeds widely. The berries aren't fully ripe. I'm a bit early to pick, since peak season is June through October, but I doubt the goddess will mind. Or even notice.

One stem yields up two or three berries, another nearly a dozen. I end up with several stems—berries and leaves and all—and carry them back to my room.

Since sunset comes at quarter to seven in early April, I make reservations for dinner at eight. An hour should be more than enough time to interview a goddess.

But what do I know? I've never done it before.

* * *

Fifteen minutes before sunset—I hate being late—I pass the registration desk where Pualani is still working. I hold up my stems of ʻōhelo berries and say, "On my way."

"Bettah go fas'," she says. "Da Park Service gonna close da Halemaʻumaʻu overlook."

"Why dey close da overlook?"

"Cuz da crater floor bulging. Maybe dey t'ink one eruption coming."

"I going." I make tracks to my car.

I head south again on Crater Rim Drive toward Halemaʻumaʻu. About half way there I pass the Jaggar Observatory and Museum where Park Service personnel are loading barricades into pickup trucks. I mash the gas pedal. Once the barricades go up, I've got no chance with Pele.

Even from a mile away I can see the smoke—a massive column spiraling into the sunset sky.

I pull in at the Halemaʻumaʻu overlook, grab my sprigs of ʻōhelo berries, and walk toward the hissing and rumbling. The sulfur smell thickens. It's hard to draw a breath.

The sun sinks to the crater's western rim. I consider turning back. But I keep walking.

twenty-seven

The first thing I see on the path to the crater's edge is this sign:

> **WARNING**
>
> STAY ON ESTABLISHED TRAILS.
>
> STAY OUT OF CAVES AND CRACKS.
>
> POTENTIALLY LIFE-THREATENING
>
> CONCENTRATIONS
>
> OF CARBON DIOXIDE.

I'm hiking just to the overlook—only a short distance on the three-mile Halemaʻumaʻu Trail—but I make a mental note and look around. The landscape is rock. There's nothing green. Smoke from the crater keeps billowing. The hissing and rumbling grow louder. I move on and pass another sign.

The "Firepit" of Halema'uma'u

Halema'uma'u Crater is the site of the most eruptions at the summit of Kīlauea Volcano. Between 1905 and 1924, a period of about 20 years, a dazzling lake of molten lava circulated within its walls. Then, in 1924, the lake drained away, allowing groundwater to penetrate deep inside the volcano. Enormous steam explosions resulted, showering the landscape with rocky debris, still visible around the rim today.

When the floor of the pit abruptly rises or falls, as is occurring now, things can happen fast. I plan to be outta here if they do.

Upon reaching the overlook, I peer down. The crater is about a half-mile across and a hundred yards deep. Molten lava gurgles through cracks in the bulging floor. The fiery pool is a fraction of the whole, but it's liquid and moving. Flames lick up the crater wall. And from the flames comes that twisting column of smoke.

My eyes smart. I blink away tears.

The last beams of the setting sun flicker over the crater's edge. The sky around the sun whitens like a halo, but elsewhere darkens. Lava below in the pit takes on a crimson glow. Flames flare like torches. The molten lake becomes luminous—in the same hot hue as the flames.

By the overlook there's a small platform surrounded by a picket fence and another sign that I can barely read in the diminishing light:

> *'Āina a ke akua e noho ai*
>
> Land where the goddess dwells

Pele's home. The sign reminds me of the warning delivered to Ransom's wife moments before he died: "As you value your health and your life keep away from Pele . . . Deadly." Had he heeded that warning he might still be alive. And I would not be here.

Turns out I'm not the only one bringing her an offering tonight. Standing by the fence, a few feet in front of me, a ponytailed girl drapes a *lei* around the pickets. The fence is already festooned with half a dozen *lei.* Just beyond sits a plate of mangos and papayas and a bottle of liquor—I can't make out the label—wrapped in *ti* leaves. And on the barren earth around the plate are more *lei* and flowers, and sprigs of *'ōhelo* berries like I've brought.

Ponytail whispers several words I can't hear and one I can: "Pele." She's smiling through her tears. *Tears of joy—unlike mine?* I don't know. I'm a guy. But something has just happened here that's meaningful to her.

She's so into her feelings that she doesn't even notice me as she walks by, leaving me alone at the overlook. The sun's afterglow fades above the crater's rim. The fire pit's hue deepens. And it growls.

I feel like a fool. I'm standing here teary-eyed with these sprigs in my hand like they're flowers for a blind date. Will that seductive woman I saw in my dreams appear? *Right.* I have no idea what to say. But I don't have forever to say it. This crater could blow, or the barricades go up. Either way, I'll have to leave.

I'm about to screw up my courage when I hear another kind of rumbling in the lot. A motorcycle. A man dismounts his bike in the growing darkness and makes his way up the trail to the overlook.

Another guy? Another offering?

He struts up to where I'm standing like he really knows what he's doing. He's in black motorcycle leathers. His face is seriously sunburned. His salt and pepper beard is windswept. On his right hand, which is clutching a book, is tattooed an image of a Sunday school Jesus; on his left the words, GOD'S CHILD.

"Hello, brother," he says. "I just rode all the way from Kona." He may have ridden from Kona, but his words and appearance suggest he's from the mainland.

"Howzit," I say. I could use a little support, so I ask: "Are you here on a mission?"

"Right on, brother," he says, and holds up the book. It's a Bible. "I'm here to deny Pele exists. I'm going to say so right over this burning pit."

"It's been done." I relate to him how Princess Kapiolani defied the goddess over this same pit in 1823. Her followers warned her not to. But she did anyway and survived—a fact that put a big dent in the cult of Pele and furthered the efforts of the Christian missionaries in the islands.

"Never mind about the Hawaiian Princess. I need to do this for myself." He steps up to the picket fence. "It's a test of faith."

He opens his Bible to the first of about a dozen bookmarks. He announces: "Exodus, chapter twenty." Then he shouts: "'I am the Lord thy God, who have brought thee out of the land of Egypt, out of the house of bondage. Thou shalt have no other gods before me.'" He lists various forbidden idols and graven images, adding Pele to the lot, and then shouts: "'Thou shalt not bow down thyself to them, nor serve them, for I, the Lord thy God, am a jealous God.'"

The fire pit grumbles. Lava shoots into the air.

He flips pages to his next bookmark and says: "Deuteronomy, chapter eight." He shouts: "'If thou forget the Lord thy God, and walk after other gods, and serve them, and worship them, I testify against you this day that ye shall surely perish.'"

More thunder. More fountains. He turns to another bookmark and says, "Leviticus, chapter twenty-six. Again he shouts: "'Ye shall make no idols . . .'"

The ground shakes like an earthquake.

I'm afraid the crater's ready to blow. And I haven't said a single word yet to Pele. Meanwhile this guy has maybe ten bookmarks to go. It's not my style to argue with complete strangers about religion, but I have only one shot at this offering to Pele, and he's making it impossible.

"Hey, brah. You have your god," I hear myself saying. "Why not let Hawaiians have theirs?"

But he turns back to the fiery pit and shouts: "Pele, you false god, you have no power over me. You have no power over anyone. I dare you to show yourself—"

A lava jet shoots into the darkness.

He slaps his Bible shut, turns, and starts back to his motorcycle. He's not four strides from me before I know we're in trouble. Another fountain goes off. The ground shakes again. Then more jets. Soon a shower is coming down on my head. A shower of ash.

I toss my ʻōhelo berries over the fence onto the edge of the pit. "For you, Pele." Then I hear myself saying: "If you're real, show me a sign."

I run for the lot, catching up to the bearded biker as he mounts his ride. Ash is falling thicker now. Pebbles the size of hail ping on the tank of his bike, making little dings in the metal. Then pebbles give way to rocks.

"So long, brother," he says. When he starts his motorcycle, a rock the size of a baseball cracks his helmet and he tumbles to the asphalt lot.

"You okay?" I ask.

He struggles to his feet, looking dazed. "Pele is the whore of Babylon!" he seethes.

"I thought you said she didn't exist?"

He gives me a sour look, hops back on his bike, and rolls away. I run across the lot to my rental car, sure it's dinged beyond repair from the fallout. I don't take time to look. I just hop in and tear away.

As I motor to the Volcano House, out of harm's way, racing toward me are two Park Service trucks with flashing lights and those barricades stacked in back. They're closing the overlook. I may be the last person to make an offering to Pele for a long time to come.

Back at the Volcano House I carefully check the roof, trunk, and hood of my rental car. This could cost me.

Not a single ding. *Impossible.*

twenty-eight

Flying from Hilo Friday morning I notice vog still hanging over the Honolulu skyline. Pele has followed me home.

Back on Maunakea Street my message light is blinking. CAITLIN RANSOM. She's anxious to see me this morning. I return her call and she tells me she'll be here in thirty minutes. Then I sift through the stack of mail that arrived while I was away. There's a check from Donnie. She's paid me in full and included a generous tip. A sticky note attached to the check says, "Mahalo, Kai." That's it.

Before Caitlin arrives I pull out my interview notes to review them. My eyes wander to this morning's paper lying unread on my desk. The front page nearly knocks me off my chair.

A Fourth Death at Pele's Hands?

Kona: Another former officer of defunct Ransom Geothermal Enterprises was found dead yesterday in Waikoloa near the Mauna Kea Resort. The body of Michael "Mick" London lay on a barren stretch of volcanic rock near this west-side resort. Investigators say London had been fishing on the craggy coastline when he apparently fell and struck his head. Alcohol may have been a factor.

Mick London formed his own drilling supply company in the late 1980s that sold exclusively to his former employer. When Ransom Geothermal ceased drilling operations on the Big Island, London's firm went into receivership. Litigation followed in which London claimed Ransom owed him thousands of dollars on leased and purchased equipment, but London failed to prevail in court.

Rex Ransom was found dead in a steam vent at Hawai'i Volcanoes National Park in March. Two other officers from his firm, Stan Nagahara and Karl Kroften, also died in or around the park in the past two years. London's death yesterday makes four.

Each man's connection to the controversial geothermal project in the Wao Kele O Puna rainforest has persuaded some devotees of Pele that the legendary goddess of volcanoes has taken revenge.

Caitlin Ransom is early again. She's in a floral print dress that does nice things for her grey eyes. No handshake this time—businesslike or otherwise. She just slides gracefully into my client chair.

I show her the headline. She's already seen it.

"It's so sad," she says. "Mick was really a nice guy. After he and my dad had their falling out, Mick's life has been so miserable."

"I talked with him three days ago," I say. "He was broke and bitter, but very much alive."

"Did he shed any light on my father's death?" She chokes a bit on the word "death."

I summarize my interview with Mick. And then with Sonny Boy. I mention seeing her mother, but I spare Caitlin the details. I also spare her my encounter at the Halemaʻumaʻu Crater. And I keep the found lipstick to myself, for now.

"And what are your conclusions?" Caitlin asks.

I tell the hard to believe, but equally hard to reject story that Serena Barrymore, a.k.a. Goddess Hiʻiaka, told me. "She claims she saw the same woman in red I did pursuing your father on the Crater Rim Trail. Barrymore says she also saw this woman push him into the steam vent."

"But isn't Barrymore an escaped mental patient?"

"True," I say. "Not the most reliable of witnesses."

"Who could the woman in red be?" Caitlin furrows her intelligent brow. "And why would she want to hurt my dad?"

"The woman can only be Pele, or someone made up to look like her. Trouble is, I interviewed every potential suspect, and none of them even remotely resembles her."

"Leaving only Pele?" Caitlin says.

"Afraid so. Or someone not on our list who's good at costume and make-up. Maybe someone involved in the protests who's willing to kill for Pele."

"Who? I can't think of anyone," Caitlin says "But it's some comfort that you're ready to admit my father's death wasn't an accident. At least now I'm not alone."

"There's three of us," I say. "You, me, and a woman who's certified insane. We need more to go on. Can you think of other people who might have wanted to harm your father?"

Caitlin draws a blank.

I try a different tack. "Maybe your father mentioned someone or something in your last conversations with him?"

She comes up with a few things that don't sound promising. Then she says: "He said more money was coming."

"More money?" I perk up. "What did he mean by that?"

"Remember I told you he sent me a generous check?"

I nod.

"Dad said he was sending more. Both to me and to my two brothers. He said it had to do with estate planning, or something like that."

"Did you receive another check?"

"No. My brothers didn't either."

"What about your father's will? Do you know what it says?"

"No. We never discussed that. I just assumed he left everything to Donnie, since my mother's estate eventually goes to my brothers and me."

"It might be worth checking into."

"I'll do that," she says.

After Caitlin strides from my office it's almost noon. Time to leave for my appointment with Ashley at a shop at Ala Moana

Center called Safari. She's supposed to show me photos of the Lindquist twins celebrating their twenty-first birthday, before Fireball drove them off the Pali. I'm not hopeful her photos will be much use. Still, I head down the stairs.

Mrs. Fujiyama is sitting at the *lei* table with Chastity and Joon. No Blossom. Is she still in my apartment? This morning I came straight from the airport to my office, so I don't know.

I ask and Mrs. Fujiyama slowly shakes her head. "She go back to him."

"Back to Junior?" I shake my head too.

"He know she staying wit' you," Mrs. Fujiyama says. "He get furious mad. He say he gonna kill her. And you."

I'm alarmed that Blossom has gone back to Junior. Not for myself. But for her.

"You bettah watch out," my landlady says.

Before I can get out the door, his black pickup truck pulls up. The passenger door opens and Blossom slinks out. She's crying. He shouts at her before she closes the door. "I be hea at six. You be ready!"

Blossom runs from the black truck as if she's fleeing a coiled snake. He squeals away. Though it may make me late to my appointment with Ashley, I stop. Blossom looks up at me and I see a fresh bruise on her cheek. She looks down again, ashamed.

"I'm sorry, Blossom," I say. "Your staying at my place was a mistake—*my* mistake. Junior got the wrong idea."

"I tol' him you like one uncle to me," she explains. "But he no belief'."

"Uncle?" I say, surprised to hear myself referred to that way.

Then she surprises me even more. "'Nuff, awready!" she raises her voice. "Junior not going to hurt me anymo'."

Encouraged by the first inklings of a changed attitude—from victim to survivor—I don't know what to say. So I settle for, "I'll be back in an hour. Then let's talk."

She nods.

twenty-nine

Ala Moana Shopping Center at lunchtime is a zoo. Throngs of people patronize this place—the largest open-air shopping mall in the world. And they're all driving in circles right now with me, looking for a spot to park.

I hate to be late. It's already noon. Maybe Ashley won't mind—or notice.

At last I find a spot on the street level near Macy's at the Diamond Head end of the center, climb to the mall level, and head *Ewa* toward the luxury outfitter called Safari. I rush past some of the center's nearly ninety eateries and two hundred stores—mostly high-end icons like Louis Vuitton, Tiffany & Co., Chanel, Ralph Lauren, and Neiman Marcus—seeing more tourists inside than locals. I finally show up at Safari, across from Long's Drugs, huffing. It's ten minutes after noon. I hope Ashley hasn't already left for lunch.

I dash across the swanky hardwood floors and plush area rugs, and gaze at the elegant casual threads like you'd take on a big game hunt. Nice stuff. *And pricey.* Images of lions and giraffes and elephants grace the pastel walls, but

I would bet none of these duds are going on safari. Except at Disneyland.

Two young women are working the floor. One is a jaunty strawberry blonde in a pink polka dot dress. The other is in dark gothic mode—with powdered white face, red lips, and jet-black hair. I glance back and forth between the two, befuddled. Then I take the easy way out. I ask a guy behind the register, "Which one is Ashley?"

He points to the blonde. Makes sense. She appears to be about the same age—twenty-one—and from the same crowd as the late Lindquist twins.

"Sorry I'm late," I say, making my way to her. "The parking lot's a zoo."

"That's like *way* funny!" She laughs. "Are you Kai?"

I nod. She apparently thinks I'm a comedian.

"I'm Ashley." Her giddy green eyes and tiny freckles across her nose have *adorable* written all over them. "I brought my camera with the party photos." She turns down the corners of her sweet smile. *"So sad."*

"Should we go outside?" I ask.

"Totally," she replies. "It's my lunch break."

She heads for the store entrance and I follow. She's tall and wispy and sort of skips along. Her pink polka dot dress hangs on her and sways as she moves, continuing her carefree theme. She totes a handbag the size of a shopping cart, also pink. I'm hoping her camera is inside that cavernous thing—like she promised. I'm not optimistic.

Across from the store entrance, in the center of the open-air promenade, benches for weary shoppers surround a koi pond. Inside the pond the bright, patchy-colored ornamental carp swim lazily. I join Ashley on one of the benches.

I start off nice and easy. "How was your trip to Denver?"

"Kind of crazy," she says.

"Because you lost your cell phone?"

"Yeah, that . . ." She pauses. "But mostly 'cause I like found out when I landed about Heather and Lindsay. I was totally shocked, you know? And I felt *so* guilty. Like it was my fault. If I'd been there, Freddie wouldn't have driven them. He was *way* drunk."

"It's not your fault. The twins made the decision to ride with him. Those left behind often blame themselves."

"You're *way* cool, Kai. Thanks."

"If you don't mind my asking, who is Ethan and how did his phone number get into Fireball's—er, Freddie's—glove box?"

"Ethan?" she looks puzzled. "Oh, he's just a guy I stayed with in Denver. I wanted the twins to have his number, okay? But when I said goodbye to them I like forgot. So I wrote it on a receipt I found on the floor at the club and, you know, gave it to Freddie."

I nod and wonder again if she's telling or asking me.

"I really don't know how the number got into his glove box," she says. "Did he like put it there, or maybe they did? Whatever."

"Do you know whose receipt it was?"

She shakes her head. "The club was totally crowded. It could have been like anyone's."

"Probably doesn't matter now." I sigh. "But that reminds me. I've got something of yours." I pull from my pocket the bent Hawaiian bracelet with her name engraved on it.

"Oh-my-god!" Her mouth drops open as she takes the bracelet. "Where did you find it?"

"At the wreckage site—at the foot of the Pali."

"No way!"

I shrug. "Any idea how it got there?"

"I dunno," she says vaguely. "I was like showing it to some people at the club. I took it off and handed it around—okay?—and just sort of lost track of it. Later, on the airplane, I looked at my wrist and wondered, 'Where's my Hawaiian bracelet?' *Duh!*"

"Any idea why it might have been in Fireball's car?"

She looks puzzled again. "Maybe the twins found it and were like going to return it to me, or something?"

"Could be." Two potential pieces of evidence—the phone number and the Hawaiian bracelet—come to nothing. I'm wondering if the pics Ashley promises will turn out the same. I ask, "May I see your photos?"

"Totally!" She digs into that cavernous pink bag. Her fingers search like terriers. She pulls out her long-lost cell phone. "No, that's not it." Then she digs up a small leather purse. "No way." She continues digging. "I just know I put my camera in here this morning. *Really.*"

My hope is fading.

"Wait! Here it is!" She extracts a small digital camera of the point-and-shoot variety. She fiddles with the little buttons. "It's new—okay?—and I like really don't know how to use it yet."

"Take your time. No hurry."

She finally gets it turned on. An image appears. It's an ocean scene. I can see what looks like the Lindquist twins on a beach. More fumbling, and Ashley manages to scroll through the photos. One after another. More of the same. The twins on a beach. I'm getting impatient. And worried.

"*Oh, no!*" she says.

"What's wrong?" I'm fearing the worst.

"I put the wrong card in the camera. *I totally forgot!* The card with the party pics got filled, you know, so I put in another half-full card with a trip Heather and Lindsay and I took in February to Lāna'i. We stayed at Mānele Bay Resort. See?"

She shows me a photo of the three of them in bikinis on Lāna'i. Behind them dolphins frolic in bright blue Mānele Bay.

"You say there are photos of the party on this card?"

"I *think* so," she replies slowly, like she's unsure. "But most party pics are on the other one."

"Where's the other card?"

"In my apartment, I think." Then she scowls. *"Oh-my-god!* I hope I didn't leave that card in Denver!"

"Me too. Do you mind if I see the pics of the party that are on this card?"

"That's cool." She gives me the camera.

I rush along, hoping to find images of the twins' birthday party. One shot after another shows pretty much the same things. Beautiful bay. Beautiful bikinis. But none of the birthday party.

I'm about to give up. I'm about to quit when one photo freezes my attention. It's not from the party. It's another from Mānele Bay—dated in mid-February.

"Who's this?" I point to a couple—a man and a woman lying cozily together by the resort's swimming pool. The couple is in the background. One of the Lindquist twins poses in front of them.

"It's Lindsay," she says.

"No. I mean these two behind Lindsay."

"I don't know. But I remember them—he looked *way* younger than her. And they were like totally going at it. *Gross!* We felt like telling them to rent a room."

"I know the woman," I say. "She probably did rent a room. But I wouldn't have put her in it with this man. Whoever he is."

"Do they have anything to do with Heather and Lindsay?"

"I doubt it, but I'll follow up anyway. May I borrow the card?"

"Sure," she says. "Do you want to see the other one too, with the party pics? I'm totally sorry I didn't bring it. *Duh!*"

"Don't be too hard on yourself. Would you please call me when you find it?"

She agrees. "For now, here's this card." Ashley hands it to me, returns the camera to her pink handbag, and ambles back into Safari.

I clutch onto the card like it's solid gold. The woman in the photo is Donnie Ransom.

thirty

The photo poolside at Mānele Bay would have been taken a month before Donnie's husband died. I remember her telling me she spent a few days on the Pineapple Isle while her husband was undergoing tests at Wilcox Hospital. But she didn't mention she spent them with another man.

The photo calls into question everything she has told me. And the younger man she's lying with at Mānele Bay—longish dark blond hair, expressive eyes, and compact, muscular physique—gives her ample motive for not wanting her husband around.

Ashley's photo may be a game changer—though not in the game I had anticipated. The strawberry blonde who can't keep track of her own bracelet and cell phone and camera cards has come through like a queen.

Who is the man in the photo? How long has Donnie been seeing him? Did they scheme together to get her husband out of the way?

I'm mulling over these questions as I drive back to Maunakea Street, walk into the *lei* shop, and head for the stairs.

Then I see Chastity and Joon and remember that I promised to talk with Blossom. She's not there.

"Went to lunch," Joon says.

"Latahs," I say and climb the stairs.

First thing I do in my office is to slip Ashley's photo card into the appropriate slot in my laptop, open the image of Donnie and the unknown young man, and print it on a full size sheet. It comes out well. Ashley apparently has been shooting with her new camera on highest resolution, though I doubt she knows it. It's a good thing. If I can find anybody who knows this guy, there will be no problem identifying him.

On a hunch I phone Caitlin. She answers on the first ring. I don't ask her to drive across town again from the university to my office. I offer to come to her. She says she's just seen her father's lawyer on Bishop Street and is now having a coffee at Starbucks on nearby Merchant Street—only a ten-minute walk from my office.

"Will you be there for a while?" I ask.

"Sure, I just ordered a latte. What's up?"

"I've got a photo of somebody to show you."

"A photo of whom?"

"That's what I hope you can tell me."

"And I've got something to share with you," she says. "Something my father's attorney said."

"Sounds promising," I say. "See you in ten."

I hang up and start out the door with the photo of Donnie and her new man. I stop and go back inside. I grab an old pair of scissors and carefully cut the photo. When I'm done, there's a hole in the sheet where Donnie used to be. I leave her on the desk. Then I pull from the top drawer the warning note Donnie told me she received moments before her husband died. I put both the note and the photo in a file folder and head for Starbucks.

I shuffle along through Fort Street Mall, feeling suddenly beat. It's only April and it must be eighty-five. Then I remember I awoke before dawn at the Volcano House, drove to Hilo, and flew home to Honolulu before breakfast. It's already been a long day. And it's only mid-afternoon. But I feel suddenly energized by the break in the case. I don't know where it will lead, but at least I'm getting somewhere.

My breath keeps time with my quickening pace. I cough. Vog. It just won't go away. I cover my nose and mouth with my handkerchief. Then I breathe easier.

Inside Starbucks, Caitlin is not hard to find. She stands out from the other patrons—well-dressed downtown types, on break from their office jobs. Caitlin appears more casual and nonchalant. Yet more elegant. As if looking good is easy.

I say hello and put the enlarged photo—minus Donnie—on Caitlin's table. I don't want her to see her father's second wife with the younger man. Not yet. No telling how she'd react if she suspected Donnie.

"Do you know this man?" I point to the boyish figure sunning by the pool at Mānele Bay.

"Yes, but what does he have to do with anything?" Caitlin sips her latte.

"I don't know yet," I say. "Who is he?"

"Jeff," she says matter-of-factly.

"Jeff who?" The name doesn't ring a bell.

"I guess most people call him Jeffrey. He's the guy who rents the suite over the garage at my dad's and Donnie's place on Kāua'i."

I put on my poker face. "Jeffrey Bywater? Donnie told me about him. He's a flight attendant and has a partner named Byron. Jeffrey's gay, right?"

"That was my impression," she says. "But why are you showing me his photo? Does he have anything to do with my father's death?"

"I don't know," I repeat. Then I ask her what she knows about Jeffrey.

Caitlin, it turns out, has met Jeffrey only once and knows little more than I do—though she recalls he acted recently in an amateur theatrical production on Kāua'i. She thinks he's been renting from her father for about one year, and before that he lived on O'ahu.

"Did he know your father or Donnie before he moved in?"

"I don't think so," she replies.

"Thanks," I say. "Now I need you to promise me something, Caitlin. I need you to promise that you will not tell anyone I showed you this photo, and most of all you will not tell Donnie or Jeffrey. In fact, it would probably be best if you didn't speak to them at all. At least, for now. Okay?"

She nods. "I have no need to talk with Donnie anyway. And I don't really know Jeffrey."

"Mahalo," I say. "I better get working on these new leads." I rise from the table. "I hope to have some answers for you shortly."

"Wait," she says. "Don't you want to hear what my father's lawyer told me?"

"I do." I sit down again.

"His name is Sheldon Weller from Weller, Matsumoto, and Ching," she says. "He's an estate attorney and his office is in that big tower on Bishop Street right over there." She points skyward.

"So what did Mr. Weller say?"

"He said a few months ago my father phoned him about sending money gifts to my brothers and me and—"

"Do you think that's why you got the check?" I interrupt her. It's a bad habit.

"I think so," Caitlin says. "But more interesting, Mr. Weller said my father also talked about changing his will."

"Changing his will how?"

"Everything in the existing will—my dad's Hanalei home and his money—goes to Donnie, like I assumed. But my dad mentioned something to Mr. Weller about adding my two brothers and me as beneficiaries. Mr. Weller and he didn't discuss particulars, but they planned to talk again. My dad died before that could happen."

"That is interesting." I say. I don't mention it's even more interesting that his second wife was by then already hooked up with a new man.

* * *

On the way back to my office I stop at King Magazine in Fort Street Mall. It's a nondescript little red brick shop with dozens of magazines in its windows. You might just walk by without noticing, unless you're shopping for something to read. In which case, King Magazine is the place to go.

I step up to a rack containing newspapers from the various Hawaiian Islands—*Honolulu Star-Advertiser, Maui News, The Garden Island, Hawaii Tribune-Herald,* and so on. The *Honolulu Weekly*, a free newspaper, is outside in a stand by itself. From my folder I take the note Donnie said she received moments before Rex Ransom died. I have only a photocopy, but I remember the words were pasted on common white paper with no fancy threading or watermark.

A note like this seems a bizarre tactic in the digital age. But it makes sense. Hard copy is more difficult to trace. It leaves no electronic trail. The official investigation apparently found no usable prints on the paper or pasted letters. The maker obviously wore gloves.

I glance again at the note.

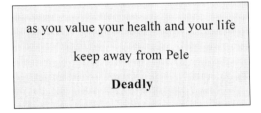

as you value your health and your life

keep away from Pele

Deadly

The wording sounds quaint and bookish. Most people would say, "*if* you value your health" not "*as* you value . . ." Or was "as" simply handy and whoever made the note just slapped it down?

All the words appear to have been cut with scissors from a newspaper, except the word "Pele," which I recall from the original had the glossiness of a travel brochure. White correction fluid has been applied to cover glue smudges. Whoever made the note was a neat freak. And probably didn't make it on the fly—but with premeditation. I doubt the note originated at the Volcano House.

Four different fonts, of various sizes, make up the newsprint words. I check these fonts against those in the islands' newspapers. The *Hawaii Tribune-Herald,* the obvious choice, looks similar, but not really the same. *Hmmm.* Maybe the *Star-Advertiser?* It's available on all islands. The *Star-Advertiser* is close, but no cigar. I step outside and check the *Honolulu Weekly*. It doesn't work either.

Now it's anybody's guess. I come back into the shop. The *Maui News* looks like a prospect, but it too doesn't work. That leaves *The Garden Island*. I check its various fonts. They all match.

The Kāua'i newspaper.

I walk up Fort Street Mall to my Maunakea Street office, considering what I've learned. Donnie Ransom is not what she appears to be—devoted wife of her elderly, wealthy and now deceased husband. She's a cheater whose lover is the Ransom's own tenant, Jeffrey Bywater—though Bywater presents himself as gay. Maybe Ransom suspects his wife is unfaithful. Maybe his suspicion, coupled with his renewed closeness to his three children by his previous marriage, is his motivation for phoning his estate attorney and discussing listing them as beneficiaries. Changing his will means Donnie would get less—maybe a lot less.

I recall harsh words between Ransom and his wife at the Volcano House—so at odds with the public image of them as a loving couple.

"What about me? I'm your wife!" Donnie had exclaimed.

"You have nothing to worry about," the old man had replied.

Could this exchange have been provoked by Ransom's intention to change his will?

Back in my office I call Donnie Ransom.

"Kai?" She sounds surprised. Then she says perfunctorily: "How are you?"

"I'm fine," I say. "Thanks for the check and generous tip."

"You're welcome," she says.

"I wanted to convey my sympathy, again, and tell you how sorry I am about your husband."

"That's very thoughtful of you," she says. "Very thoughtful."

"And I also wanted to mention that I'll be on Kāua'i tomorrow and I wondered if you'd mind if I stopped by."

"Mind? No, I don't mind." She sounds puzzled. "What's up?"

"It's about your husband—a final detail I'd like to clear up for my records."

"Can we talk about it on the phone?" She's looking for a way out. I'm not giving it to her.

"We can, but in person is always better," I say. "What time is good for you?"

"Uh," she hesitates, "early afternoon."

"Thanks, I'll give you a call before I come. *Aloha.*"

Donnie is cooperating with me—reluctantly. I expected she would.

I call Hawaiian Airlines and book a flight to Lihue on Saturday morning, returning later the same day. And I line up a rental car.

I'm about to do something unorthodox—*again.*

thirty-one

Saturday morning I fly to Lihue and drive the Garden Isle's meandering two-lane Kūhiō Highway to Hanalei. The home of the late Rex Ransom sits right on the pristine beach and has a commanding view of Hanalei Bay. The sprawling oceanfront residence is every bit as grand as I imagined it would be.

It's a little after noon when I arrive, so I grab a couple Spam *musubi* in the village, carry them down to the beach, and plant myself in the warm sand. As I bite into the grilled Spam and rice wrapped in *nori,* or dried seaweed, I watch the waves and remember why Hanalei is one of my favorite spots in the islands.

Hanalei must be other people's favorite spot too. Maybe that's why it's been featured in so many films. Millions who've never had the good fortune to set foot here have set eyes on images of this lovely little bay, covered pier, and lush mountain backdrop in *South Pacific, Lilo & Stitch, The Descendants,* and many more. Though the bay is small, it has several breaks: Waikoko on the west side, Hanalei Pier in the center, Hideaways on the east side beneath the cliffs by Princeville Resort, and so on. I've got no board today, and a job to do, so I can only watch.

My Spam *musubi* gone, I phone Donnie and then walk up the beach to the Ransoms' home. It's not every day a private detective calls on a former client and accuses her of murder. I'm not going to do that, exactly. I plan to soft-pedal the thing.

Mainly, I want her to know that I know. My hunch is Donnie will say or do something hasty or desperate that will help the case along. Maybe not today. But soon. I still don't know how she and Jeffrey did it. I could use some assistance. It's a bit risky. But I'm betting the benefits outweigh the risks. If I'm right, I'll come off looking good. If I'm wrong, I may wipeout big time.

Why not let law enforcement take over from here? Simple. Given the circumstantial evidence against them—some of it sounding outright wacky—Donnie and Jeffrey could easily slip through legal loopholes. And if they were to stand trial, it's anybody's guess whether twelve jurors would convict. If not, the two would walk. And get away with Ransom's murder and his millions.

There's a FOR SALE sign in front of the house. Already. I check out the suite over the three-car garage where I assume Jeffrey lives. Or *lived.* I bet he's moved into the main residence by now. A pair of jogging shoes by the front doors, shoes too large for Donnie's delicate feet, seems to confirm this. But I'm not surprised when she meets me alone at the door.

I'd forgotten how attractive she is. Even greeting me casually in her own home, she maintains that beauty queen aura. Her lustrous black hair, her vivid brown eyes, and her inviting red lips make it easy to see why the late Rex Ransom and the late Mick London both fell hard for this island beauty. And at least one man before them. And one man after.

"Thanks for seeing me," I say.

"I'm curious," she says, as she leads me into the elegant home. "What are you doing on Kāua'i?"

"Working a case." I leave it at that and look around. More evidence of Jeffrey: A baseball cap embroidered *Pride of Aloha* on a chair. A half empty beer bottle on an end table that strikes me as male carelessness. I've never seen this home before, but I can tell at least two people reside here.

She leads me into a huge living room that looks out on the sunny beach where I've just been warming myself in the sand. All that blue water and blue sky in the windows reminds me of the late Rex Ransom's other home in Kona, now occupied by his first wife, Kathryn. *Two dream homes and he can't enjoy either.*

Donnie and I take matching leather chairs beside an inlaid *koa* table.

"Sad to see you're selling your home," I say.

"Yes," she replies. "Too many memories of Rex. I've got to move on."

"I understand."

"I miss that man," she goes on. "It's painful each day to live here without him."

"I'm sorry." I play along. "Where will you go?"

"I don't know," she says vaguely. "I haven't decided yet. One step at a time. First sell the house."

"I talked with your late husband's daughter recently," I say, getting to the point.

"Oh?" Donnie says.

"Caitlin asked me to investigate his death. She's not convinced it was an accident."

"Really?"

"Yes," I say. "I went back to the Big Island, interviewed people, and checked about everything I could check."

"And what did you find?"

"Nothing. Unless we can believe Pele did it."

Donnie gets a funny look. "So what do we have to talk about?"

"It turns out I'm working on another case. I told you about it—the Pali case."

She nods, but still looks confused.

"One witness in that case," I continue, "took photos in the Honolulu club where the twins and their driver were last served—probably over-served."

"Now I'm really lost," Donnie says. "What does this have to do with Rex?"

"Stay with me," I say. "So this witness brings the wrong photo card to our meeting. It's got no photos of the clubs, only an earlier trip to Mānele Bay on Lāna'i."

"So?" Donnie looks suspicious.

"One photo taken at the Mānele Bay Resort I thought you should see." I haul it out and she takes it.

When she recognizes herself lying by the pool with Jeffrey, Donnie's face freezes.

"The date," I say, "is February twentieth—about three weeks before your husband died. Was that when he was having the tests you told me about at Wilcox Hospital?"

I assume by the strained expression on her face that she's working fast to concoct a story.

She finally speaks. "Look, Kai, Jeffrey and I are friends, okay? He helped me cope with Rex's first heart attack. It changed everything."

"I'm sure it did." I sympathize.

"Jeffrey happened to be working a flight to Lāna'i when Rex was having those tests, and we sort of ran into each other at the hotel. That's all."

"I expected it was something simple like that," I say. "I'm glad you explained. I was concerned, you see, about the impression the photo might make if," I pause, "well, if the official investigation were reopened."

She strains again, but manages no reply.

"You can have the photo." I hand it to her, confident she'll show it to Jeffrey. "No worries," I say. "You were with me when your husband died. And Jeffrey was on a cruise ship, right?"

"That's right," she says. "You can check it out—and I wish you would. I don't like either of us being suspected."

"I'd be happy to do that, if it would make you feel better. And I'm sure I'll find it's just as you say."

"*Mahalo*, Kai," she says.

I'm walking along the beach to my rental car and turn around for one last look at the Ransoms' oceanfront palace. Through the sea-view glass I see Donnie already on the phone—probably talking to her partner in crime. I can almost read her lips: *"Jeffrey, he knows!"*

Suddenly I realize why the color of her lips looks so familiar. *Fiery red.*

thirty-two

I'm back on Maunakea Street late on Saturday afternoon. Chinatown shops are already starting to close. Including Mrs. Fujiyama's. *Pau hana*. I'm about to close up shop myself. But not before I begin to check out Jeffrey's alibi.

The *Pride of Aloha*. I have no doubt Jeffrey was booked on the interisland cruise ship with his supposed partner, Byron Joslyn, just as Donnie claims. Why else would she have brought it up? So I don't need to see a passenger list. But it might be worth checking the cruise ship's schedule and ports of call.

I Google *Pride of Aloha*. I hit a site that gives a bunch of statistics about the ship. As a *keiki* I marveled at the immense size and grandeur of the ill-fated *Titanic*. The *Pride of Aloha* is even bigger—longer, wider, and heavier. The website shows a real-time satellite image of the liner and its position. From the heavens, where the satellite is perched, the huge white vessel looks like a toothpick in a puddle. But guess what? It's in port in Honolulu at this very moment. The *Pride of Aloha* is moored by the Aloha Tower. *Five minutes away.*

I get the brilliant idea to buzz over to the Aloha Tower and see if I can corral a real live person into talking to me about the ship. I drive down Bishop Street, wait for the long light at Ala Moana Boulevard, and then cross into the parking lot at the Aloha Tower Marketplace.

I can't miss the *Pride of Aloha.* It dwarfs the marketplace, rising nearly as high as the tower itself. A colossal white floating hotel. I crane my neck and gaze up at its countless decks with balconies and suites, and as many portholes below those decks. There's quite a crowd in the long covered concourse beside the ship. Passengers are milling around or in queues boarding the liner. By the huge doors and gangways swallowing them up, white-suited officers are checking documentation as one after another climbs aboard.

I know little about how the inter-island cruise operates, what schedule it follows, and how it accommodates passengers. I need to learn fast.

Another white uniform is roaming the concourse in what appears to be a hostess role. I approach her and say, "Aloha, would you please help me?"

"Did you complete your online check-in form?" she asks.

"I'm not boarding the ship tonight," I say. "I just have some questions."

"Would you like a brochure?" she asks. "It has the ship's schedule and frequently asked questions."

"Sure. That would be a good start."

She hands me the brochure. I step aside and scan it. On the front is a photo of the great white ship, cruising in dazzling teal waters between the islands. The *Pride of Aloha,* the brochure says, has over 660 balcony staterooms, eight restaurants, three pools, spacious public rooms and meeting facilities, a tennis court, and an art gallery. Plus a Hawai'i-themed Aloha Cafe and Waikīkī Bar.

Sign me up! I'm ready to sail. Except for the fare.

This kind of travel seems designed for those with a bank account like the late Rex Ransom's. Curious that a guy living in Ransom's garage could afford it.

The back of the brochure lists the ship's interisland cruise schedule. The schedule is unchanging. The liner departs from Honolulu on Saturday evening at 7:00 pm and follows the same itinerary, week after week. Sunday and Monday in Kahului, Maui. Tuesday in Hilo. Wednesday in Kona. Thursday and Friday in Nāwiliwili on Kāua'i. Saturday morning, back to Honolulu.

Interesting. The *Pride of Aloha* spends two nights each week, Tuesday and Wednesday, in Big Island ports. When Rex Ransom died on a Wednesday morning near the Volcano House, the ship was just arriving in Kona, after sailing overnight from Hilo. Jeffrey Bywater could have disembarked in Hilo on Tuesday and driven to the park, spent the night near the Volcano House, murdered Ransom on Wednesday morning, and then driven to Kona and re-boarded the ship.

The perfect crime and the perfect alibi. How he managed to pull it off is another question. But clearly Jeffrey had the opportunity.

I return to the hostess in white with a question: "If I take the interisland cruise, can I disembark in Hilo, explore the Big Island on my own, and then re-board in Kona?"

"Absolutely," she says. "As long as you re-board at least one hour before sailing time."

"Will I need to sign out when I leave the ship, and sign in when I return?"

"Yes," she says. "But it's very simple and quick. When you first board you'll receive an ID card, about the size of a credit card, with your photo and personal information in digital form. You'll use the card in many ways, from making onboard purchases to accessing your room. And also for boarding and disembarking the ship in ports of call. Whenever you disembark you simply swipe the card in a reader by the gangway, a crewmember double-checks that it's you swiping the card, and you're off. It takes all of about ten seconds."

"What about getting back on the ship?" I ask.

"Same procedure," she says. "You swipe your card again, the crew member double-checks, and you're in."

"Mahalo," I say. "Very helpful."

But I'm wondering: *How did he do it?* How could Jeffrey get off the ship at Hilo and then re-board the next day in Kona without being detected? I assume Donnie would not invite me to check out her lover's alibi unless it were ironclad. It's not easy to subvert digital ID cards, especially under watchful eyes. And I wouldn't think it's any easier to disembark other than by the gangway. A first-rate professional might pull it off, but could Donnie's lover?

"May I book your cruise?" She smiles and hands me her card with a gauzy image of the ship.

"Let me check with my better half," I say.

She glances at my left hand—without a ring—and looks dubious.

"For our honeymoon." I make tracks for the door.

As the *Pride of Aloha* readies to sail into the sunset, I head back to my office. The *lei* shop is closed, so I climb the outside stairs. First thing I do is send an email to Pualani at the

Volcano House. I attach the photo of Jeffrey Bywater and Donnie Ransom.

"Evah see dis guy?" I ask in my email message. "He maybe stay in da Volcano House when Ransom *huli* inside da steam vent?" Then I close with *"Mahalo"* and leave her my cell phone number, in case she prefers to call.

I don't know if Pualani is working tonight, or how often she checks her email. I figure it may be Monday before I hear from her.

Almost instantly my cell phone dings. *Pualani? Already?*

No. It's a text from Maile. She wants to know if I'm taking Kula surfing this weekend. I haven't been in the water for days. Plus it's weekend and I just drooled over the rippling breaks at Hanalei Bay. I text back, "For sure."

"When?" she texts back.

"Tomorrow a.m.," I reply.

"Can u pick him up tonight?"

"OK."

"Kula in back yard," she replies.

That's it. While I'm stoked Maile texted me, I'm a little surprised at the arrangements. I've never picked up Kula at night before. Dogs are technically not allowed at the Waikīkī Edgewater. Maile knows the rules. That's part of the reason she adopted Kula and I didn't. So I'm a bit mystified. But I hop in my car and head up into Mānoa Valley.

My cousin Alika's thirteen-foot tandem board sits in Maile's carport—ready to go. I don't knock on the cottage door, even though there's a light on inside. I walk straight to her back yard, cursing Madison Highcamp under my breath, and call, "Kula."

He doesn't come.

It's dark. I can't see him. But I call him again. "Kula!"

Still no golden retriever.

Now I'm scratching my head. What's going on? She invites me to take the dog surfing, tells me he'll be in the yard, I come promptly as if called like a dog, but there's no Kula.

So finally I go around to the front door and knock. "Maile?"

"Come in," she says, as if she's expecting me.

I step into the cottage. Coconut, Peppah, and Lolo are lounging in their usual places. Kula's toys are scattered about the floor. But no dog.

Maile is sitting in her rattan loveseat in a strapless dress—rare for her. Her hair is down and shimmering.

"Maile?" I say. "Where's Kula?"

"Oh, Mrs. Lee asked if Kula could walk with her and her Labrador retriever. Kula goes crazy when he sees that lab," Maile says. "Do you mind waiting?"

"No, I don't mind," I say, glad for the opportunity to see her, whatever the excuse. My phone rings and I direct the call to voicemail.

"Would you like to sit?" She gestures to the rattan chair opposite her, occupied by Coconut.

"Sure." I move toward the chair. The Siamese jumps down and joins Maile on the loveseat.

"I was at the Waikīkī Canoe Club today with a client whose Siberian husky I recovered," Maile says, "and I ran into your paddling buddy, Nainoa."

"Nainoa? I haven't seen him since—" I stop midsentence. Nainoa introduced me to Madison Highcamp.

"Nainoa mentioned that drunken woman you knew who phoned me. I told him about the call and he said it was all a lie."

I'm about to say, *That's what I've been trying to tell you!* But instead I just make a mental note: *Buy Nainoa a six-pack.* My phone beeps indicating a new voicemail. I let it go.

Soon Maile and I are talking more like we used to—easy, comfortable, familiar. The animation and color return to her face.

When Mrs. Lee finally returns with Kula, he runs to me with that big goofy smile. I stroke his golden coat.

Maile pipes up, "What about that dinner you promised me, Kai Cooke?"

"Ah Fook okay?" It's the chop suey house in Chinatown where Maile stood me up after receiving Madison's drunken call.

"You're on." She feeds the animals and we go.

A few hours later we're back in her cottage, full and happy. I remind her that dogs aren't allowed at the Waikīkī Edgewater—and hope she'll get the hint.

"I'm feeling so much closer to you now, Kai," she says. "But we've been a long time apart. I'm not quite ready."

She's not quite ready, I'm thinking. *And I'm so ready.*

"But you can sleep here," she continues—and I perk up— "on the loveseat with Peppah. That way, you won't have to sneak Kula into your apartment."

"Thanks." I glance at the male Angora lounging on the loveseat and try not to show my disappointment. *Her feelings run deep,* I console myself. *It's going to take her a while.*

Maile disappears into her bedroom with Kula—*lucky dog*—but returns to the living room in her robe a minute later. I'm slipping off my aloha shirt.

"I missed that, you know." She fixes her eyes on my shark bite—the crescent of sixteen pink welts. "Funny, it makes you kind of—*vulnerable.*"

"I'll give you a private showing when you're ready." I wink.

"I'll look forward to that," Maile says and returns to her bedroom.

I climb onto the loveseat and curl around Peppah. Things could be worse. He's very soft. And at least I'm sleeping in Maile's cottage.

In the middle of the night I get up to use the bathroom and take my phone. There's that new voicemail—the one that came earlier in the evening. I listen.

"Hey, Kai," Pualani says. "Da guy in da picture—das da guy I wen tell you 'bout—Stapleton."

Stapleton? I wonder.

"Lars Stapleton from New Jersey." She sounds like she's reading the hotel register.

So Lars Stapleton equals Jeffrey Bywater.

Pualani goes on: "Stapleton da guy wen insist fo' crater view room numbah t'ree. Remembah?"

I remember. Next to room one—the Ransoms' room. With the connecting door between. Jeffrey—*Lars*—would have checked out before Ransom died and fled afterwards to re-board the *Pride of Aloha* at Kona. Just time enough to do the deed, but not enough—as he told Pualani—to view the eruption.

"Eh, Kai, what dis Stapleton guy doing in da picture by da pool wit' Mrs. Ransom? He her new boyfrien'? She no waste time, brah!"

Her boyfriend, yes. But not exactly *new.*

Pieces of the case start coming together. But the piece that still doesn't fit is that mystery woman. Donnie Ransom and her lover Jeffrey, a.k.a. Lars Stapleton, somehow manage to field a young Pele lookalike on the Crater Rim Trail, assisted possibly by Jeffrey's supposed partner Byron Joslyn. I don't know yet how they do this, or how Jeffrey disembarks the *Pride of Aloha* in Hilo and re-boards in Kona without being detected. But I hope I'll find out soon enough.

When I climb back onto the loveseat Peppah is gone and sleep doesn't come. It's not just Rex Ransom's murder I'm thinking about.

Donnie planned to make her husband's death look like the third in a string of deaths at Pele's hands. Three in a row is convincing. Four in a row, even more. *Mick London.* Did Donnie conspire to kill him, too?

Maybe Mick knew too much? He told me Donnie liked Ransom's money more than she liked him. Maybe he suspected his former boss's death was no accident. Jeffrey, an interisland flight attendant, could easily find himself in Kona with a few spare hours between flights. Donnie—presumably single again—could tag along and show up at Mick's place, have a few drinks with her former beau, and leave the rest to Jeffrey.

Two counts of murder instead of one?

thirty-three

Sunday morning after Maile and I breakfast together I take Kula surfing. We drive down Mānoa Valley, his head out the window, his fleecy fur glowing in the morning sun. He's wearing that goofy smile again. *Revved up to surf!*

Kula is beside himself when I turn *makai* off Ala Moana Boulevard into Kaka'ako Waterfront Park. The golden retriever hears the waves crashing beyond the dune and smells the salt spray. He wants to ride waves. Before we do, I power up my phone. It's been off since last night. There's a new voicemail.

"Easy, boy." I try to calm him. "Just a minute while I listen to this message." *Like he really understands?*

But he does. He sits quietly on the seat next to me. I dial my voicemail and hear Ashley's voice.

"*Way* stupid!" She chides herself. "I found that other photo card in my bag. It was there like the whole the time! *Duh!* Can you believe that?"

Yes I can.

She'll be working at the mall if I want to come by, 10 to 5. I'll return Ashley's call after I set up an interview with Jeffrey's friend, Byron Joslyn. First Byron, then Ashley.

Once Kula sees the phone call is over, he goes ballistic. I grab the tandem board and we hike over the dune to the water. In the break two surfers are sitting on their boards.

Kula jumps on the tandem and walks to the nose. I hop on behind the retriever and paddle to the break. The two surfers spot a set coming and paddle for it. When the first shoulder-high roller comes, they're on it. And ride it all the way in.

We watch a few more waves roll through. Then we go for one. I swing the board around and point the nose toward shore.

"Okay, Kula," I say. "Here we go."

The golden retriever hunches down, poised to ride. I paddle and Kula hangs his paws over the nose. Soon I feel the rush under the board of the cresting swell. I pop up and turn right, staying in front of the breaking wave. Kula balances himself and keeps in sync with me as I maneuver on the wave. It's like he has a knack, or something. I hear myself sounding like Ashley. *Gag me!*

While Kula and I wait for the next wave I worry about my vocabulary. And I think about Jeffrey's friend, Byron Joslyn. What might Joslyn's role be in Rex Ransom's murder? Was he a willing co-conspirator? Or an unsuspecting bystander—just along for the ride? It's hard to imagine him not being at least minimally aware and involved. You'd notice if your traveling companion went missing overnight. How much he was involved may determine his willingness to talk. I'm hoping he runs off at the mouth.

When I return Kula to her cottage after our session later that Sunday morning, Maile isn't home. I bathe the golden boy, dry him, give him food and water, and leave him in the yard. He's smiling at me when I close the gate and walk to my car.

On Sunday morning the *lei* shop is closed. I climb the outside stairs to my office and I Google Byron Joslyn. He has an address and phone number in Pauoa, the little valley along the town-side of the Pali Highway. I call the number and a woman answers. I ask for Byron. She tells me he's working a trip from Seattle and will be back this afternoon.

"He's still a flight attendant?" I ask, putting two and two together. "I haven't seen him for a while."

"Yes," she says. "Can I tell him who called?"

"An old friend," I say. "So did Byron finally tie the knot? Are you his lucky bride?"

"Me?" She laughs. "I'm not his type. We're housemates. We work for the same airline." She mentions the airline. It's the one Jeffrey works for too. That's all I need to know.

So I say, "You've been very helpful. I'll give Byron a call when I'm in town again. *Mahalo.*"

I hang up, go back on line, and check Sunday's flight schedule on Byron's airline from Seattle to Honolulu. Only one flight departs Seattle, at 12:50 pm, and arrives in Honolulu at 3:45 pm.

I check my watch. 11:30 am. I call Ashley. She doesn't answer. I leave her a message that I'll see her at noon at Safari.

Before driving to Ala Moana Shopping Center I burn a CD containing the images from her photo card. I put the card in a file folder for the Ransom case and take the CD with me. I'm feeling the Bishop Street attorney who represents the Lindquist twins' father breathing down my neck. Plus, racer-boys like

Fireball who drive drunk, and the clubs that serve them when they're already drunk, need to be held accountable. I'm hoping this time Ashley comes through.

Parking is even worse on Sundays at Ala Moana Center than on weekdays. I finally find a spot, race across the mall to Safari, but step into Long's Drugs first. I buy a photo card identical to the one Ashley lent me and a lipstick that looks like the one I found on the Crater Rim Trail. Shoving the lipstick into my khakis for later, I cross the promenade to the gleaming hardwood floors of Safari. *Late again!*

Against the images of lions, giraffes and elephants that grace the pastel walls, I don't have to search long this time for the strawberry blonde. But she looks astonished. She says something to her gothic co-worker and then meets me in the middle of the store.

"Sorry I'm late again," I say. "The parking lot's a zoo, but this time no excuses."

"Late?" Ashley says. "Like for what?"

"Didn't you get my voicemail?" I'm incredulous.

"Um . . . no," she says. "I totally lost my cell phone again." Her giddy eyes turn a deeper green.

She lost her cell phone—again?

"I guess I just like left it, you know, somewhere," she explains. "I'm sure it'll turn up. I really haven't looked yet. Whatever."

"Good luck," I say.

"I found it last time," she says. "Well . . . uh . . . the airline found it. But I did find the other photo card. *Really!*"

"Great," I say. "Should we go outside?"

She nods and leads the way in her lanky carefree strides to the benches around the koi pond. She lugs her oversized pink handbag that I hope contains the photo card she's promised me. We sit by the pond.

"Before I forget," I say. "Here's a new photo card to replace yours, plus all your photos on this CD. I hand her both.

She doesn't question my keeping her own card. She just says: "Did that totally gross couple by the pool have anything to do with Heather and Lindsay?"

"I'm afraid not." I tell her the plain truth.

"Um . . . I didn't think so," she says. "I can still remember those two like really going at it. And I remember them saying some really weird stuff."

That gets my attention. "Like what?"

"She said this weird thing to him about Pele."

"Madame Pele, the goddess of volcanoes?"

"*Bizarre* . . . them lying there all wrapped up in each other—*Gag me!*—and talking about the volcano goddess."

"Can you remember what she said about Pele?"

"Something about revenge—like it was time for Pele to take revenge."

"What did he say—the guy?"

"He said, 'Anything you want, baby, you got it.'"

Hmmm. I scratch my chin.

"*Baby?*" Ashley says. "She was like twenty years older than him!"

I grab the spiral notebook I carry in the pocket of my aloha shirt. "Would you mind writing down what they said and how they were behaving?"

"Whatever," she says.

With the pen I also keep in that same pocket I write the date of the overheard conversation and the place at the top of the page. These will be corroborated by the dated photo

Ashley gave me. I hand her the notebook. She records the conversation as she remembers it and describes Donnie and Jeffrey lying together poolside. I also have her state that she gave me the photo card, to establish chain of custody. She signs and dates her statement and returns the notebook to me.

"Mahalo," I say. "This could be a big help."

Ashley doesn't ask why. She just smiles and digs into her huge pink handbag. She digs and digs. Another puzzled look. Then she says, *"Oh, no!"*

"Oh, no?" I say, expecting the worst.

"The photo card." Ashley says. "It's like not here."

"I thought you said you found it last night?"

"I did," she says. "I found it and set it on my nightstand before I went to sleep, you know, just to make sure I would bring it today. I guess I like didn't put it back in my bag."

"So you don't have the card?"

"Yes . . . um . . . I do have the card." She frowns. "Just not with me."

I shake my head. But manage to hold my tongue.

"I'm totally sorry," she says. "Especially since, you know, I like forgot the card last time."

"It's okay," I hear myself say. "Could I meet you at your home maybe later today?"

"Oh, *barf!"* she says. "I can't. I'm going to Maui with some friends right after work. I'll be back on Tuesday."

"Tuesday?" I grab for some patience. It's hard to find. Finally I say: "Same place, same time on Tuesday."

I walk her back to Safari and she says, "No way I'll forget this time—*like I promise!"*

And I'm thinking: *Like I hope so.*

thirty-four

Back in my office I get on my computer again before driving to the airport to meet Byron Joslyn. I jot down the number of his flight from Seattle, the arrival gate, and baggage claim area. What I don't have, yet, is a mug shot.

I Google Byron Joslyn again. I get hits from ancestry.com and sites like that dealing with deceased and historical Byron Joslyns. *Who'd have known there were so many?* Why am I wasting time? I go to Facebook.

Two Byron Joslyns come up. Only one resides in Honolulu. And he has an uncanny resemblance to Jeffrey Bywater. The two look like brothers. There's a shot in Byron's photo gallery of the two of them arm-in-arm. Byron must be older. He's got features like Jeffrey's, but not his boyish looks. Byron's personal information says he's in a relationship. The implication of the photo is that the relationship is with Jeffrey. If so, it's not an exclusive one.

I look at Byron's list of friends. It includes Jeffrey, of course. And also Donnie Ransom. And checking his gallery again, I spot photos of all three of them arm-in-arm.

But what most impresses me is that uncanny resemblance of the two men. One could probably pass for the other. So I Google Jeffrey Bywater to see what I can find. I go to one of those public records sites that says it will supply dozens of records pertaining to Jeffrey Bywater if I pay $14.95. I don't usually pay for this kind of information, but I'm in a hurry and I'll take my chances. So I key in my credit card number and see what comes up.

There's quite a bit. Mostly addresses and previous addresses. A divorce about five years ago. I'm wondering if I've wasted my fifteen bucks. But then I see this: NAME CHANGE. Jeffrey Bywater is not his given name. He changed his name barely one year ago. And guess what? His given name is Joslyn. Jeffrey Bywater and Byron Joslyn don't just look like brothers. They *are* brothers.

On a hunch I Google Jeffrey Joslyn. The first hit is a review in *The Garden Island* of an amateur performance at the Pohu Theatre in Lihue of Oscar Wilde's *The Importance of Being Earnest*. I recall Caitlin's mentioning that Jeffrey acted in a play on Kāua'i. It appears he's kept his real name as his stage name. The review goes on and on about the controversial and daring move by director Nani Michaels of casting male actor Jeffrey Joslyn as a leading lady.

> Jeffrey Joslyn, in the role of the beautiful and pretentious Gwendolen Fairfax, who embodies the qualities of conventional Victorian Womanhood, is bound to raise eyebrows. The young Gwendolen—fixated on finding a husband named Earnest—played by a man? But Joslyn pulls it off swimmingly. He nails the

> speech, mannerisms, grace, and charm of the
> twenty-something Victorian beauty so com-
> pletely that you forget almost instantly he's
> cross-dressing and raising his voice an octave . . .

"You forget almost instantly he's cross-dressing." That line sticks in my mind. And suddenly it's so clear.

Jeffrey Bywater—a.k.a. Jeffrey Joslyn—is an accomplished amateur actor, especially accomplished at convincingly portraying young women. It was him I saw in his next role: the beautiful young *kinolau* of Pele on the Crater Rim Trail.

I don't bother with the other hits on Jeffrey Joslyn. I've found what I need. By now it's approaching three. Byron's flight arrives in forty-five minutes. I shut down my computer, take the business card of the *Pride of Aloha* staff who assisted me, and head for Honolulu International Airport.

I park near baggage claim area G, where passengers from Byron's Seattle flight will collect their luggage. And that's where the crew will most likely pass. I'm early, but I've never known a flight to arrive exactly on time. Often airplanes catch a tailwind to Hawai'i and arrive ahead of schedule. I can't risk missing Byron Joslyn.

I walk from the garage to baggage claim. The arrivals board says that Byron's Seattle flight has indeed landed early. Passengers begin streaming down an escalator and through sliding glass doors near where I'm standing. As bedraggled moms and dads with their yawning kids stumble in, I keep an eye out for the first sign of the flight crew.

As baggage claim fills, behind the throng the crew begins to emerge. Women flight attendants. Two pilots. More attendants. And finally a woman and a man walking together.

The man is Byron. He's put on weight since his Facebook photo, but Jeffrey's features still shine through. I follow Byron through baggage claim and out the glass doors to ground transportation and the parking garage. He and the woman part company. Then I walk up to him.

"You look familiar," I say. "Did you recently sail on the *Pride of Aloha?*"

"Yes," he says. "Were you on the cruise?"

"I work for the cruise line." I show him the *Pride of Aloha* business card, but pull it back before he can see the name "Margo" on it. "I'm waiting for some VIPs arriving on a flight from San Francisco."

"I don't remember seeing you on the ship," he says.

"I'm in customer relations," I say. "I don't very often sail."

"*Too bad.*" He sounds sincere.

"But I can't believe my luck." I deliberately perk up.

"What luck?"

"Well, I do the post cruise interviews after each sailing and it's often a pain to track down our customers after they disembark. But here you are!"

He looks at his watch. "How long will it take?"

"Only a few minutes," I say. "I have to meet that Frisco flight."

"Okay," he says. "Make it quick?"

"Quick it is." I point to a bench overlooking the endless stream of cars and cabs and buses gobbling up passengers and their belongings. We sit. I pull out my pen and spiral notebook, glance at his nametag, and write "Byron."

"Do you mind giving me your last name?" I ask.

"Joslyn," he says.

"*Mahalo,* Mr. Joslyn," I say. "So you took the cruise—when was it—the week of March 13?"

"Uh," he thinks for a moment, "that's right."

"And did you travel alone or with someone?"

"With someone. A friend of mine."

"Fantastic," I say in my best impression of a cruise consultant. "Did you both enjoy the cruise?"

"We did. Very much."

"Wonderful." I beam. "Did you take advantage of any on-shore activities at various ports?"

"Some," he says.

"How about on the Big Island, for instance? Did you and your friend disembark at Hilo or Kona?"

Byron hesitates. "Uh, I did," he says. "Both ports."

"And your friend?"

"Uh, no," Byron says. "He wasn't feeling well—a touch sea-sickness."

He's lying. But I know now how Jeffrey Bywater left and returned to the *Pride of Aloha* without a trace. Is Byron lying to hide his brother's relationship with a married woman, or to hide his brother's murder of her husband? The way Byron's blabbing, he's either stupid or he doesn't know everything.

"Where did you go on the Big Island?" I let him dig himself deeper.

"Oh, the usual attractions," he says vaguely.

"Then you must have seen the eruption in the Halemaʻumaʻu Crater?" I throw him a curve. There was no eruption on those days.

"Yes, I sure did." He looks at his watch again. "Amazing."

I take the hint. "Thank you very much. *Pride of Aloha* is pleased you had a fun-filled cruise. And we hope to welcome you back again soon. You may receive a follow-up call asking you about our conversation. I'd appreciate if you'd give me positive feedback."

"I will." He taps me on the shoulder. "I know how it goes in the travel industry."

"Oh, could you tell me where I might find your friend to interview him?"

"He's also a flight attendant," Byron says. "And I happen to know he has Monday off. But he lives on Kāuaʻi."

"That's not in the budget, I'm afraid." I rise, say *"Mahalo,"* and walk away.

Now I can piece it all together.

Jeffrey Joslyn, a.k.a. Jeffrey Bywater, boards the *Pride of Aloha* on Saturday with his brother, Byron Joslyn. The ship calls at Hilo on Tuesday morning. Jeffrey disembarks using Byron's ID, rents a car probably as Joslyn, drives to the Volcano House, and stays in the room next to Rex and Donnie Ransom under the assumed name, Lars Stapleton. Donnie and Jeffry communicate through the rooms' common doors. Wednesday morning Jeffrey impersonates Pele on the Crater Rim Trail, approaches and startles Ransom, and then hurls him into the steam vent. Jeffrey ditches his costume, carelessly drops the red lipstick along the trail, drives to Kona, and re-boards the *Pride of Aloha* using Byron's ID.

Finally, to help sell Ransom's death as Pele's revenge, Jeffrey and Donnie return to the Big Island and kill Mick London, making it appear that he falls on rocks while fishing drunk.

This sounds convincing enough to me. But would it to a jury? There is little solid evidence. Though Jeffrey was identified by Pualani at the Volcano House, no trace of him or his costume turned up on the trail, except for the lipstick that lay in the sun, mist, and rain for several days. Not to mention that the key witness—who claims she saw the crime being com-mitted—is an escaped mental patient.

Not enough to convict anyone of anything. Yet.

Back to Hanalei.

thirty-five

Monday morning before I fly to Kāua'i I gather all my notes and evidence for the Ransom case into a Manila envelope and slip it into my top desk drawer. Then I call Tommy. He's not in yet—he's probably sleeping off a late-night gig—so I leave him a message.

"Tommy, if you read about my untimely demise on the Garden Isle in tomorrow's paper, use your key to my office to recover an envelope in my desk pertaining to the Ransom case. You were right. Donnie has a new lover—Ransom's tenant, Jeffrey. She and the tenant killed the old man. Make sure you nail them. And make sure Ransom's kids get their rightful inheritance. If Donnie and Jeffrey really do go after me, that should clinch the case." I pause, wondering if I've forgotten anything. I give him Caitlin's phone number and then conclude, "Oh, yeah—if I don't come back you can have my '69 Impala."

Then I call Caitlin and also get her voicemail. "I'm wrapping up the investigation with one last neighbor-island trip," I tell her. "If I'm not in touch with you on Tuesday, please call my attorney, Tommy Woo." I give her his number and explain he will keep her posted in the unlikely event I am detained.

On the flight to Kāuaʻi I realize I've willed Tommy the one thing of value, besides my surfboard, I own. Imagine. Thirty-four years on this earth and my only possessions worth passing down are my board and a classic clunker that dates back to the moonshot.

From Lihue Airport I aim my rental car up the meandering Kūhiō Highway. Around Anahola I get behind a truck belonging to Oshiro Produce. On this narrow, winding road there's no chance of passing the big rig. So I follow the pineapple painted on the back until the truck finally turns off at the Princeville resorts. By then I'm on the even narrower and slower Highway 560 approaching Hanalei, and have to wait for oncoming traffic at the one-lane suspension bridge over the Hanalei River. The trip takes twice as long as it should, but no matter.

I park a few doors down from the Ransoms'. I'm back in Hanalei for the same reason I was here before. Last time I worked on Donnie. This time, Jeffrey. My hunch is he's not as smart as she is. And twice as arrogant. I'm not going to soft-pedal this time. And I'm betting he's going to do something desperate. Sooner rather than later.

Main thing: I don't want to see Donnie and Jeffrey walk. I don't want to see them get away with Ransom's murder and his millions—while his own children not only lose their father but also their inheritance. In the unlikely event anything happens to me, Tommy will follow through.

In the driveway are two new vehicles with temporary plates: a black Range Rover and an Audi convertible in the metallic red of Fireball's mangled Honda, but with more sparkle. Donnie and Jeffrey didn't waste time buying new toys. I knock on the door.

Jeffrey Bywater appears. We've never met, but instantly he knows who I am. And instantly I see why Donnie cozied up to him. He is—in person, as in his photo—a beautiful boy. His eyes are even more expressive than in the Mānele Bay pic. And his dark blond hair and trim muscular physique more striking. He's easily a dozen years junior to the widow of Rex Ransom. Now I can see how he passed for a young woman on stage and at Hawai'i Volcanoes National Park.

I don't expect him to invite me in, so I stand by the open door and say, "You dropped something on the Crater Rim Trail." I pull from my pocket the red lipstick I bought at Long's Drugs.

He glances at it. His eyes show a flash of recognition.

I toss him the lipstick.

He reaches for it. Then reconsiders and lets it drop. "You almost got me," he says. "You want my fingerprints—don't you?"

"I don't want your prints," I say. "That's not why I'm here."

He looks puzzled. Then he says, "Beat it, Sherlock, before you run into somebody more clever than you."

"Okay, but just one question before I go," I say. "I know you killed Rex Ransom . . ." I pause. "That's not my question. You had the old man believing you were gay, while you and his wife waited for him to die so you could collect his millions. But when you found out he planned to change his will, you hatched a plan for him to die mysteriously in Pele's domain, like two of his former executives. You arranged ironclad alibis. Donnie would be with me at the Volcano House. And you would be on the *Pride of Aloha* with your brother, whose last name is different—since you changed yours."

"No shit, Sherlock." He smiles smugly. "Any moron can find name changes on the internet."

"You talked your way into the room at the Volcano House adjoining the Ransoms and made yourself up like Pele. So far, so good. You even fooled me."

"You're not much of a detective, Sherlock." The more he talks, the less I like him. And I didn't like him much to begin with.

"But you made some mistakes. Like lying poolside with Donnie at the Mānele Bay Resort. Like leaving this red lipstick," I gesture to it on the doormat, "along the Crater Rim Trail. Like pasting the warning note from newsprint in *The Garden Island*. And trusting your brother not to talk. There's more. But that's enough for now."

The first inklings of doubt cross his face. Will he call me Sherlock again? He doesn't.

So I say, "But my question isn't about Ransom. It's about Mick London." I pause again. "How did you and Donnie kill him?"

"Mick was drunk," Jeffrey says. "He slipped on a rock."

"I think he had help."

"You can't prove that," he says. But the way he shifts his weight from one foot to the other makes it seem like he's getting worried.

"She cast a spell over you, Jeffrey. She's a granite lady and you're a putty man. You wanted her so badly you'd do anything for her. Maybe that can be your plea deal."

The words barely get out of my mouth when Rex Ransom's widow strides to the door. Her beauty queen smile is gone. In its place is a dark, malicious grin. Her sparkling eyes now look like knives. She's scary.

"So long, Jeffrey." I step back. Enjoy your last days of freedom." Then I gesture to the red lipstick on the doormat. "So long, Donnie. You can keep the lipstick. It's your color."

Five minutes later I'm driving along the Hanalei River and the taro fields that border Kūhiō Highway doing forty-five—a good clip on this narrow, shoulder-less country road. As the hairpin turn and one-lane bridge approach, my rear view mirror is suddenly filled by a Range Rover—big and black and coming fast.

The Rover's motor roars. I feel a jolt from behind and hear metal grinding.

My car lurches forward and my speedometer climbs. *Fifty. Sixty.* I glance again at the mirror. Donnie is behind the wheel. Jeffrey is riding shotgun. Their faces show desperation. Looks like I got what I wanted. And it's not a pretty sight.

The hairpin and bridge are coming. No way I can make either at this speed.

But that's the idea. And that's the price I pay for taking a risk. They think I'm the only one who can put all the pieces together. They think I'm the only one standing between them and Ransom's millions. They don't know about Tommy.

My speedometer climbs. *Seventy.* That hairpin approaches. The push on my bumper suddenly eases. Donnie swings the big black Rover around on my left—against the flow of traffic. Lucky nobody's coming. She slams the Rover into the driver's side of my car. I hear another crunch of metal. She's trying to push me into the river.

I fight back. I crank my wheel to the left, against her. We careen down the highway—filling both lanes—locked in a battle that, odds are, I'll lose. My right wheels are already off the road.

The bridge arrives. But it's no longer empty. That Oshiro Produce truck I followed up from Anahola to Princeville crosses and turns onto the highway. The driver sees us coming.

Doesn't matter. There's nowhere he can go—except head-on into the Rover. I slam on my brakes and hear the impact. Both the truck and Rover sweep behind me. My car slides sideways onto the bridge. It bangs the steel rails on either side. But makes it across.

I pull off the road and run back on foot. The wreckage lies on the Hanalei side of the bridge. A few cars have stopped and people are jumping out and hurrying to the scene. Some are talking excitedly on cell phones.

The Oshiro Produce truck looks okay from behind. Its dual wheels are still firmly under it. But the cab is crunched. Miraculously the driver is moving inside. He's talking to a bystander and pointing to his arm. The trucker apparently thinks it's broken. If that's all that happened, he's lucky.

Donnie and Jeffrey aren't so lucky. Through the Rover's shattered glass I see their unworn seatbelts hanging from the bent B-pillars. Inside the crushed cabin is a mess. Nobody is moving. Not even the bloodied and now deflated airbags could save them. Donnie is slumped over Jeffrey. They are locked in a last fatal embrace.

thirty-six

Tuesday I'm in my office reading the morning paper.

Two Dead in Kāua'i Head-on Collision

Lihue: A head-on collision yesterday on Kūhiō Highway claimed the lives of two Kāua'i residents and injured a third. According to Kāua'i police, a black Range Rover heading from Hanalei toward Princeville crossed the center-line when attempting to pass another vehicle near the one-lane bridge over the Hanalei River and collided head-on into a truck owned by Oshiro Produce. Both occupants of the Range Rover—driver Donnie Ransom, 47, and passenger Jeffrey Bywater, 29, of Hanalei—were killed. Neither was wearing a seat belt. The driver of the truck, Elton Yashima of Anahola, was admitted to Wilcox Hospital in serious condition, but has since been upgraded to fair.

Excessive speed may have been a factor in the accident. Police estimate the Rover was traveling in excess of seventy miles per hour in a forty-five zone. Her Hanalei neighbors identified Donnie Ransom as the widow of the former CEO of Ransom Geothermal, who died recently at Hawai'i Volcanoes National Park. Jeffrey Bywater was a tenant in the Ransom home.

I was at the scene when Kāua'i police and EMS arrived. After the produce driver was taken to hospital and Donnie's and Jeffrey's bodies were removed, I gave a statement to police. My statement was corroborated by my badly damaged rental car and by the truck driver when he was interviewed later that day. There remained little doubt about Donnie and Jeffrey's desperate attempt to silence the only person who they believed could prove they murdered Rex Ransom.

Their violent deaths on Kūhiō Highway unfortunately won't bring him back, but at least Caitlin and her brothers should now be able to claim the inheritance their father intended for them.

The morning flies by. I'm pleased about closing the Ransom case. And I'm looking forward to seeing Maile. She's stopping by this afternoon with Kula and later we're going out. I'm hoping she's finally ready.

Things are looking up. Except I still haven't closed the Pali case.

Just before noon I drive to Ala Moana Shopping Center again to see Ashley. She's promised to bring her photo card with the birthday pics that I hope may move the case along.

Soon we're sitting by the koi pond, Ashley reaches into her pink handbag and—miracles never cease—extracts the long-awaited photo card. She slips it into her camera.

Ashley turns on the camera and tries to scroll through the photos. "Oh, barf, I totally messed up!"

"Messed up?" I'm expecting the worst. *"Totally?"*

"Duh. I must have pushed the wrong button or something."

"So you've got no photos after all?" My hopes are fading.

"No photos," she says, "but I have this, you know, really long video instead. And look—*way* cool!—it's stamped with the date and time just before I left the party."

She's right. The date is early on Sunday, in the wee hours, about forty minutes before the estimated time of the fatal crash.

Ashley starts the video. She looks a little less perky as the images start to roll. One of the partyers is saying to a stumbling Fireball, "You're like really hammered, dude!" He gives her an odd look but seems incapable of a verbal reply. Then a woman appears in the frame with a tray of draft beers. It's Stormy, the same server who sold beer to my underage helper, Nicholas. Stormy hands a beer to Fireball and says, "That's the last one for you, pal." He takes the beer. Then she says, "You're not driving, right? He shakes his head. She replies, "You better not." She walks away.

I've seen enough.

"May I borrow your camera for a few days?" I ask. "I promise to return it."

"Whatever," Ashley says. "Is the video what you need?"

"It is."

I thank her, have her write another chain of custody statement in my notebook, and walk her back into Safari. Then I drive to Maunakea Street feeling relieved. Now I have a dated video that shows Fireball being served when he's obviously drunk, and the server, Stormy, appearing to acknowledge that fact. With this I've got something Mr. Lindquist's attorney should be able to use.

More than I could have hoped for.

Back in my office I call the attorney and he's pleased. It's turning out to be a good day. I phone Tommy with the news.

Tommy answers, "Howzit, Kai?"

"What—no joke?" I'm stunned.

"I'm not in a laughing mood." He sounds down. "The wedding's hit a glitch. Zahra may have to go back to Kenya."

"How come?"

"Long story," he says. "Meet you for dinner tonight? Same old place?"

"Sorry, I'm going out with Maile. How about tomorrow night?"

"Okay," he says.

"You don't sound good, Tommy. Sure you're alright?"

"I'll survive." He hangs up.

I'm feeling suddenly gloomy as I close up my office and walk down the shag stairs. The atmosphere inside the *lei* shop doesn't help. Blossom's ex-boyfriend, Junior, is back. He's shouting at her and Mrs. Fujiyama is picking up the phone.

Junior rips the phone base cord from the wall, nearly knocking Mrs. Fujiyama down.

Then Blossom rises from her chair, defiantly looks him in the eye, and shouts, "Get outta here, Junior! Leave me alone!"

Junior lunges over the *lei* table at her, but I grab him from behind and hurl him down onto the floor. He rolls around on the linoleum, looking dazed. He glances up at his ex-girlfriend standing resolutely by the lei table, and then at me standing over him with fists clenched. No trash-talk this time. Junior pulls himself up, lumbers from the shop, and screeches away in his truck.

A post-traumatic silence descends on the shop. After her display of bravery, Blossom looks stunned. She clutches me and buries her suddenly tear-streamed face in my chest, darkening my aloha shirt.

At that moment Maile steps into the shop with Kula. When she sees Blossom wrapped around me, Maile's mouth drops open. The color drains from her face. She turns and stalks out of the shop, leaving the golden retriever behind.

I pry myself from the *lei* girl and run after Maile. "Wait!" I shout. "Maile, it's not what you think!"

"I don't want to hear it, Kai Cooke." She turns around. "You just burned your last bridge." She runs down Maunakea Street.

I chase after her. Kula pulls up beside me and then darts ahead after Maile. I grab his collar. Maile crosses the intersection at Pauahi Street. By the time we get there, the light turns red. Traffic whizzes by in both directions. I try to restrain the retriever, but he keeps pulling.

"Easy, Boy." I grip his collar with both hands.

When the light turns green, Maile is already half way down the next block and disappears in the crowded sidewalks around Hotel Street. There's no use trying to catch her in this traffic. Not with Kula off leash. If anything happens to him—I don't even want to think about it.

"C'mon, Kula." I turn around and start walking back to my office. He plants his paws. He wants Maile. *That makes two of us.*

"It's okay, boy." I stroke his warm fur. "We'll get her back. I promise."

I coax him to the *lei* shop. Before we get there I see Junior's truck pulled over on Maunakea Street behind two HPD cruisers. They're handcuffing him and putting him in one of the cruisers. *Got him!* I wish I could be happier about it. *No good deed goes unpunished.*

Inside the shop Blossom and Mrs. Fujiyama are sitting together at the *lei* table. Blossom isn't crying anymore.

"They arrested Junior," I say. "You're safe now, Blossom."

"Oh, *mahalo*, Kai!" She hugs me and pats Kula.

Then I have an inspiration, and switch to Pidgin. "You like do me one favah?"

She nods. "Shoots!"

I give her Maile's cell number and briefly explain what just happened.

"Okay, I gonna call right now!" Blossom says. "Fo' sure!"

She pulls her cell phone from her purse and dials. Before the conversation begins—I don't want to hear it—I turn to the retriever.

"C'mon, Kula," I say, "let's get some wheels and go fetch our favorite pet detective."

The dog looks up at me, wags his tail, and the two of us head for the parking garage.

About the Author

Chip Hughes earned a Ph.D. in English at Indiana University and taught American literature, film, writing, and popular fiction for nearly three decades at the University of Hawai'i at Mānoa. His non-fiction publications include two books and numerous essays on John Steinbeck.

An active member of the Private Eye Writers of America, Chip launched the Surfing Detective mystery series with *Murder on Moloka'i* (2004) and *Wipeout!* (2007), published by Island Heritage. The series is now published exclusively by Slate Ridge Press, whose volumes include *Kula* (2011), *Murder at Volcano House* (2014), *Hanging Ten in Paris Trilogy* (2017), and reissues of the first two novels.

Chip and his wife split their time between homes in Hawai'i and upstate New York.

95201728R00128

Made in the USA
Columbia, SC
07 May 2018